Warren F. Evans

The Happy Islands

Or, paradise restored

Warren F. Evans

The Happy Islands
Or, paradise restored

ISBN/EAN: 9783744794329

Printed in Europe, USA, Canada, Australia, Japan

Cover: Foto ©Andreas Hilbeck / pixelio.de

More available books at **www.hansebooks.com**

THE
HAPPY ISLANDS;

OR,

PARADISE RESTORED.

BY

REV. W. F. EVANS.

———

BOSTON:
H. V. DEGEN & SON,
22 CORNHILL.
1860.

PREFACE.

It is the object of this little volume to analyze some of the higher forms of Christian experience, and to afford a ray of light to the thousands of God's dear children who are panting for a higher spiritual condition, and a fellowship with God which shall satisfy all the needs of their nature. The author has aimed to describe not only the interior blessedness of the higher degree of divine life in the soul, but also the influence which it has upon the appearance of the outward world. When the soul becomes united to Christ, and is restored to that

blissful intercourse and affectionate familiarity with God which was its original state,
it then, from its lofty standing ground, and
through a purer medium, sees the earth
invested with new charms. To such a soul
the world is not a howling wilderness, but
is as the garden of the Lord. Then

> " Earth 's crammed with heaven,
> And every common bush afire with God."

One of the fundamental ideas of the work
is, that what we lost in the fall of our first
parents has been restored in Christ. All the
essential elements of Paradise, so far as it
was a moral and spiritual state, may be now
regained in him ; and when Paradise is
formed within, we find the outward world
in harmony with our redeemed spiritual
nature.

The plan of the work is different from
other books on the subject of full salvation,
but it is hoped that it will, on that account,

be none the less acceptable or useful. The inward life which it unfolds is not impracticable to any one who has entered upon the incipient stage of redemption, and the author only desires that it may be reproduced in the heart of every one of his readers. Whatever of spiritual truth is found in the book is all of Christ, who is the uncreated Word and the self-existent Truth. If there is in it any thing contrary to the truth as it is in Jesus, it proceeds of course from the writer, who, though he loves truth as he loves God, yet sees only through a glass darkly. May the reader appropriate, to the progress of his soul in love and wisdom, all the truth contained in the volume. May all its error be rejected, as a healthy eye rejects a particle of earthy dust that falls into it. If it shall minister comfort to souls in distress, guide any to an all-satisfying communion with a present Deity, and assist one struggling spirit in its birth into a higher life, the end for which it was written will be gained. The work, such as it is, is humbly consecrated to God, and the good of his neighbor, by the author, whose highest ambition is to be a servant of the servants of his Lord.

CONTENTS.

CHAPTER III.

THE SUPREME GOOD SOUGHT AND FOUND.

CHAPTER IV.

THE ISLAND ANAPAUSIS, OR THE LAND OF REST.

CHAPTER V.

A DARK DAY AT THE HAPPY ISLANDS.

CHAPTER VI.

THE ISLAND OF EUPHROSYNE.

CHAPTER VII.

THE ISLAND OF PLEROPHORIA.

CHAPTER VIII.

TELEIA AGAPE, OR THE REALM OF PURE LOVE.

CHAPTER IX.

THE ISLAND OF ELEUTHERIA.

CHAPTER X.

THE ISLAND HENOTIA, OR THE STATE OF DIVINE UNION.

THE HAPPY ISLANDS.

CHAPTER I.

THE VOYAGE, AND DISCOVERY OF THE ISLANDS.

The Belief of the Ancients in the Happy Islands. — Homer. — Plato. — Plutarch. — Whence this Belief arose. — Paradise is a spiritual Condition. — How the Author was led to seek the Happy Islands. — Inward Combats and Struggles. — The Purpose formed and the Voyage undertaken. — The Land appears. — The Islands gained. — The divine Humanity appears. — Description of him. — The Condition of full Salvation. — Sinking into Life. — Testimony of Guigo. — Of Tauler.

MAN HAS always been unwilling to believe that paradise has been forever lost to the world. There has lingered in the mind of the race a yearning for its restoration, and a belief that the blissful abode of peace and innocence was still in the world, or would be restored to it. It has occurred to the author of this volume that an account of his discovery of earth's lost paradise, and a history of a few years' residence in it, would not meet with an unwelcome reception from those who, tired of outward and material enjoyments, sigh for inward repose and tranquillity.

The ancients supposed that somewhere in the ocean was situated a delightful region, free from the extremes of heat and cold, and crowned with spontaneous plenty, and the bloom of perpetual spring. This pleasant place they denominated *Insulæ Fortunatæ*, or *Beatæ* — the Fortunate or Happy Islands. Here they placed their Elysium, or the abode of the blessed, which Homer thus describes : —

> " Elysium shall be thine — the blissful plains
> Of utmost earth, where Rhadamanthus reigns.
> Joys ever young, unmixed with pain or fear,
> Fill the wide circle of the eternal year.
> Stern winter smiles on that auspicious clime ;
> The fields are florid with unfading prime.
> From the bleak pole no winds inclement blow,
> Mould the round hail, or flake the fleecy snow ;
> But from the breezy deep the blest inhale
> The fragrant murmurs of the western gale."

Plato also, in an eloquent strain, describes them in his Timæus and Critias, and makes them the seat of his ideal republic, or perfect state of society.

Plutarch informs us that a certain distinguished

Roman general, by the name of Sertorius, who, having met in Spain with some persons newly arrived from the Fortunate Islands, was so enraptured with the glowing account they gave of those happy regions, that, being quite tired out with so many fatigues and dangers both by sea and land, he resolved to retire thither, and spend his life in peace and quietness, far from the noise of war, and free from the cares of government. It was a happy exchange to leave earth's "gilded rottenness" for a solid peace and substantial bliss.

The belief of the ancients in this happy region may have been a lingering traditionary remembrance of the primitive paradise, and arose naturally from their undefined longing of soul for an unrealized good, which nothing in the old world, either in its civilization, or philosophy, or religion, could satisfy; or it may have arisen from the idea of the perfect, which lies deeply seated in the consciousness. There is in the human spirit an intuitive conviction that there exists somewhere the pure, the beautiful, and the good. This leads the soul to believe both in an earthly paradise, and in immortal and celestial bliss. It is only Christianity, when apprehended, not merely as an outward mechanism of forms, or even as a creed for the intellect, but as an interior divine life, the life of God in the soul of man, that can give rest to the deep inward cravings of humanity. The soul demands something divine, something infinite. It is only when Christianity pervades the whole being with its new light and life, and joins the soul by a tie stronger than death to its Source in the unity of one spirit, that the desires of the heart, " winged of heaven to fly at infinite," can find rest. Christ is the Desire of nations, because he came to bring in himself and in his religion all that the souls of men had ever desired. In this capacity he sublimely stood before the assembled multitude in Jerusalem on the last day of the feast of tabernacles, and cried, " If any man thirst, let him come unto me and drink." And how often did he call the restless, wandering soul to fly to him as the centre of its rest! Ever since man was driven out from paradise, humanity has cast a longing look back to that delightful abode of peace, and of man in union with God. Christianity comes to meet this longing. The Happy Islands must be sought somewhere in her domains.

Paradise, like the heaven for which the Christian hopes, is not wholly nor chiefly an outward condition. It is not a material landscape, or a golden city, or a place bounded by material limitations, which must be entered from without; but it is a spiritual condition to be developed by the redeeming agencies of the gospel from within. To enter paradise we need not move through space; we need not ascend into the heavenly worlds, nor cross on expanded wing the stellar spaces. It is an ascent only in the scale of life. It is living in God, in conscious communion and union with the infinite life and love. It is dwelling in the "limitless abode of an omnipresent Deity." This right appreciation of the nature of paradise, as an inward moral state, I find in an old author, who wrote about the year 1350, who belonged to a class of pious persons in Germany, who were called "Friends of God." (*Gottes freunde.*) He says, "What is paradise? All things that are; for all are goodly and pleasant, and therefore may fitly be called a paradise. It is said, also, that paradise is an outer court of heaven. Even so this world is verily an outer court of the Eternal, or of eternity, and

2 *

specially whatever in time, or any temporal things
or creatures, manifesteth or remindeth us of God
or eternity; for the creatures are a guide and a
path unto God and eternity. Thus this world is
an outer court of eternity, and therefore it well may
be called a paradise, for it is such in truth. And
in this paradise all things are lawful, save one tree
and the fruits thereof. That is to say, of all things
that are, nothing is forbidden, and nothing is contrary to God, but one thing only, that is, sin."
(*Theologia Germanica*, p. 173.) He who looks
upon the outward world, and all the arrangements of Providence, as an expression or visible
representation of the will of God, and with all
holy beings in the universe is enraptured with the
thought that his will is done in heaven and earth,
need not journey far to find a lost paradise. Behold it is nigh thee, it is in thee. The voyage
to the Happy Islands is not so much a movement
through space, as a movement of the soul towards
God. It was God within that made the original
paradise; and when the soul is brought back
through Christ to that primitive divine fellowship,
paradise is restored. When the human spirit is

sundered from God by sin, the whole universe becomes a hell; when it is again made one with the Deity, from whom it has broken away, the whole outward creation becomes the ante-chamber of the celestial state.

> "When God is mine, and I am his,
>   Of paradise possessed,
> I taste unutterable bliss,
>   And everlasting rest."

The author was led by various influences to go in search of the Happy Islands. He became first fully convinced that they were not merely the abode of immortals, but were somewhere in this world, and it was the privilege of even mortal men there to find rest. The spiritual state symbolized by them seemed to belong to this earthly stage of our redemption. For many years had he craved the holiness and unutterable bliss which they were supposed to afford. The experience of the primitive apostles and believers, described in the New Testament, was viewed in painful contrast with the position of the Christian life he had reached. There seemed a fulness in the divine promises he had never grasped. The sense of distance from

God became almost unendurable, and the spirit pined for a closer communion with him. Like the Roman Sertorius, he fortunately came in contact with a person who had long resided in the Happy Islands. His account of them increased the soul's inward thirst to partake of their blessedness, and begat an increasing dissatisfaction with the ordinary rudimentary experience, the infantile position of the divine life, with its mixed state of joy and sorrow, love and fear, holiness and sin.

No person ever reached his soul's supreme good, in a complete self-abandonment and union with God, without a struggle with opposing influences, and an encounter with the whole strength of his sinful tendency. The soul clings with the tenacity of a death grasp to its idols, and is reluctant to forsake the transient and perishing creatures for the infinite Creator. Doubts of the real existence of those islands would creep into the mind, insinuating that they were only in the realm of fancy, and were not a reality. They were a fable, and not a fact. These doubts were unbosomed to the person who claimed to be an inhabitant of that delightful clime. The account he gave of them was characterized by a great simplicity, and appeared such as only an eye witness could give. His words came from a heart which was the seat of deep sincerity. The arguments which were presented against him he did not refute. He did not and could not reason. He was unskilled in dialectics. Like the beloved disciple John, he did not argue, but gave the facts of a living experience. His belief was rooted immovably in his inward consciousness. Christ within had become the central point of his spiritual existence, and he could say with John, " That which was from the beginning, which we have seen with our eyes, which we have looked upon, and our hands have handled, of the Word of Life. For the Life was manifested, and we have seen it, and bear witness, and show unto you that eternal Life, which was with the Father, and was manifested unto us ; that which we have seen and heard declare we unto you, that ye also may have fellowship with us. And truly our fellowship is with the Father, and with his Son Jesus Christ." (1 John i. 1–3.) His belief was too deeply embedded in his consciousness to be dislodged from his mind. There was something in his relation of a living experience that carried conviction with it, beyond what the best constructed arguments could do. A happy repose beamed in his very features, and his countenance revealed the paradise within. He spake the language of the Happy Islands, wore their peculiar costume, and had evidently acquired their manners.

Not only doubts of the real existence of the *Insulæ Beatæ* were encountered, but it was suggested that only a few, if any, seemed interested to emigrate to them. Whoever went must go alone. Also, the land which I now occupied was pleasant. Most persons desired no better. And it was not certain that the Happy Islands were designed for all. A favored few might attain them, but the soul felt its own unfitness to dwell there. Others might reach that earthly paradise, but it was too much for every one to hope ever to gain. The thought also paralyzed the energies of the soul in undertaking what seemed so difficult an enterprise, that if one should reach them, it was not certain that he would remain there always; and then he would be more discontented than ever with his present residence. It seemed that the higher form

of life which there reigned must be exceedingly difficult. But never was there a greater mistake. It
has ever been found that the higher forms of the
Christian experience are the easiest to live. When
the whole nature is pervaded by the Christian
spirit, and its current changed in the direction of
God and heaven, the soul does right without a
struggle, without an effort. The straighter the line
of light on which the Christian walks, the easier
is his path to travel. The nearer the soul approaches in the progress of its redemption to an
angelic life, the more spontaneously it moves towards
God and in the highway of holiness. Some of the
older philosophers seem to have had an idea of
this feature of the higher life. Perhaps there were
some remembrances of the original state of man in
Eden, which were struggling with the moral darkness of the world, and which had not been wholly
swallowed up by the surrounding midnight gloom.
The following maxim is taken from a work of the
Chinese philosopher, Lao-tseu, called the " Book of
the Way and the Truth," written about six hundred
years before Christ : —

" Men of superior virtue are ignorant of their

virtue.   Men of inferior virtue do not forget their virtue.   Men of superior virtue practise it without thinking of it.   Men of inferior virtue practise it with intention."   Happy is that man whose holy life is not so much a struggle as a spontaneity.   We may also be assured that the deeper our experience of divine things becomes, and the more we partake of the divine nature, the less will be the danger of our falling away.   It is easier to fall from a mixed state than a state of pure love.   The nearer one gets to the heavenly world, and the more he is in sympathy with all holy spirits, the less is the probability that he will ever lose the life of God in his soul.   Though a liability to sin, and a possibility of departing from the right way, may always be predicated of free will in this earthly sphere, yet there is a state of comparative fixedness of character even in this life.   Mr. Charles Wesley had an apprehension of this when he wrote the following stanza : —

> "My steadfast soul, from falling free,
>   Shall then no longer move ;
> But Christ be all the world to me,
>   And all my heart be love."

When Christ becomes all the world to us, it is

hard to break away from him. When urged by temptation to do it, the soul, with a sense of the poverty of created things, and their inability to satisfy desires that aspire to the Infinite, at once demands of the tempter, " To whom shall I go ? "

If one is tempted to feel that he must start for the Happy Islands alone, and that he will find them an uninhabited solitude, it is enough that he can say with Jesus, " I am not alone, but the Father is with me." And if one feels any painful foreboding of apostasy from Christ, and that his soul may be cast upon the eternal shore a moral wreck, let him hasten from the frontier of the kingdom of God into its interior, and there, with his soul deeply fixed in God, let him forever rest.

These doubts and temptations delayed for a long time the voyage. But the restless soul cried out incessantly for the supreme good. Having conceived the idea of a holy life, and become enraptured with its moral beauty, the heart could not be contented short of its perfect realization. There was a more painful sense of the emptiness of worldly things. The soul was " blessed with the scorn of finite good," until at length it was brought to a crisis in its inward history. It seemed to be a question of spiritual life or death. Finally, free will summoned all her energies, and, concentrating all her forces into one volition, the *purpose* was formed. The question was weighed, the cost was counted, and the resolution deliberately made to start at once, and, if need be, at the loss of all things, to search the ocean through until the Happy Islands were discovered.

The first inquiry was for a vessel that might be bound thither, which could be prevailed upon to carry me to the desired port. Several seaports were visited for that purpose, but in vain. At length a voice was heard within — "Cease ye from man, whose breath is in his nostrils; for wherein is he to be accounted of?" (Isa. ii. 22;) and, "Cursed is he who maketh flesh his arm." This convinced me that the voyage must be undertaken alone and for myself. Gaining all the information it was possible to acquire, as to the distance of the isles, their longitude and latitude, and what would be necessary for the voyage, which I needlessly feared might be a long one, I embarked on board a boat named the Resolute, at a city and harbor called

Semivivum. This city and its mixed population, who were but half alive, I bade adieu forever. The boat seemed to be well built, and able to survive the fiercest storm. It appeared every way adapted to the voyage. A flag was run up to the mast head bearing the expressive motto, " *Work and Live.*" Nothing of much interest occurred for several days. I had been directed to guide my course by the Southern Cross instead of the Polar Star. My eye was kept steadily fixed on that beautiful symbol which the hand of God suspended on the midnight heavens. Constantine could not have been more affected at the sight of the cross in the heavens, before his battle with his enemies, than was I when struggling all alone with the billows of an unknown sea. At length, just as the sun was disappearing beneath the western horizon, several islands were seen quietly sleeping on the bosom of the deep, their summits gilded with the beams of the setting sun. These I recognized as the land I sought, the home of the blest, the Happy Isles of which philosophers had dreamed, and which their restless souls had longed to behold. The setting sun had given me a glimpse of them, but night settled on the deep, and they were not gained. The wind no longer filled the sails, and a deep and powerful current, like the Gulf Stream, was bearing the boat away from them. I pierced the heavens with a cry for a gentle breeze, but the colors hung down the mast. Recollecting the motto they bore, " Work and Live," I threw off all my useless clothing, and seized the oars, resolved to *work* the boat up against the current. With the most exhausting labor, the vessel only held her own. It seemed to me like what we sometimes experience in dreams, when we appear to ourselves to make the most desperate efforts to fly from some imaginary foe, but find, to our sorrow, that we do not in the least move from our position. My efforts were like the strugglings of a prisoner to break his fetters, who is only galled and pained without gaining his freedom. Such were the inward strugglings of Saul of Tarsus to acquire freedom through the law. (Rom. vii. 14 –25.) The current was too strong for my efforts. After toiling all night, the attempt to bring the boat to land with the oars was given up. My next measure was to abandon the boat and swim to the shore. Leaving all behind, clothing, provisions, and money, I committed myself to the deep. While raised upon the top of a mountain wave, the islands were seen in the distance. But the tide was going out, and, what was worse, I was well nigh exhausted, though my will clung to the principle — work and live. At length my strength was gone, and in the depth of self-despair, I ceased to work, and abandoned the idea of struggling into life. The principle so dear to my heart was surrendered. It seemed as powerless as Canute the Dane seated on the ocean beach and commanding the flowing tide to retire. Death seemed inevitable. I must sink. I ceased to struggle, calmly crying with Peter, " Save, Lord; I perish;" and with holy Stephen, " Lord Jesus, receive my spirit." Resigning my soul and its will wholly to Christ, and quitting my hold of life, and every earthly thing, in some way unknown to me, I was carried gently in the arms of a mighty billow, and left upon the shore as tenderly as a mother's love lays her infant down to sleep.

3 *

> "Strong Son of God, immortal Love,
> Whom we, that have not seen thy face,
> By faith, and faith alone, embrace,
> Believing where we cannot prove.
>
> Thou seemest human and divine,
> The highest, holiest manhood Thou;
> Our wills are ours, we know not how,
> Our wills are ours to make them thine."

Just at the point of giving up all, I found all. When the struggle ceased the land was gained. I sunk into the bosom of the Infinite Life and all-pervading Love.

Naked, faint, and destitute of all, I lay upon the beach. Soon a being, whom it is impossible to describe, stood before me, not discerned by the outward sense, but by faith's interior eye, which was unveiled to behold him. No term can better describe his appearance than the expression, Divine Man. The thick veil of sense with which the spirit had been enshrouded was rent, and his form of majestic sweetness stood disclosed before me, and his face was radiant with infinite moral beauty. He fully met my ideal of man. In all other men it was possible to find only an imperfect realization of the idea of man, like the broken and half-buried columns of some ancient temple, which were but the relics of ruined greatness. Even in the best of men I had ever been pained with the contrast between the ideal of humanity and its actual realization in their character. But here the true conception was embodied in a living personality. The rapturous love of the spouse in the Canticles has described him, where, beneath the sensuous symbol, faith must discern the spiritual sense, and where divine moral beauty gleams through the outward letter, like sunshine through an evening cloud. "My beloved is white and ruddy, the chiefest among ten thousand. His head is as the most fine gold; his locks are bushy, and black as a raven. His eyes are as the eyes of doves by the rivers of waters, washed with milk, and fitly set. His cheeks are as a bed of spices, as sweet flowers; his lips like lilies, dropping sweet-smelling myrrh. His hands are as gold rings set with the beryl; his legs are as pillars of marble, set upon sockets of fine gold. His countenance is as Lebanon, excellent as the cedars. His mouth is most sweet; yea, he is altogether lovely." (Canticles v. 10–16.)

This was an hour when faith broke through the envelope of outward sense, in which it had been incrusted and imprisoned, and gazed with unveiled face upon the more solid realities of eternal things. It was an hour to be laid up in everlasting memory. An eloquent writer has asked, " Are there not times when the soul asserts her supremacy over the earthly body, and even her independence of it, and rises into a realm of bliss and purity which the body knows not of? Yea, when the body hangs about her not only as a clog, but as a torturing rack, has she not soared upward and left it stranded, and enjoyed converse with eternal things such as it never helped her to enjoy? Apart and behind the wall of sense, have we never been caught up by high communings into that diviner sphere, where are the substances of which earth is only the shadow, —

> " As sings the lark when sucked up out of sight
> In vortices of glory and blue air ? "

Such was the hour of my landing on the Happy Islands, when He whose countenance was like Lebanon seen in the distance, a thing of unearthly beauty and quiet majesty, appeared as my Support and Guide. He filled the emptiness of my spirit with divine peace. He put upon me a robe of spotless white, as pure as the untrodden snow. Faint with hunger, weary, and sighing for repose, I said to him who had taken captive my heart, "Tell me, O thou whom my soul loveth, where thou feedest, where thou makest thy flock to rest at noon; for why should I be as a wanderer [or straggler in confusion] by the flocks of thy companions." His words flowed into my soul like music from a celestial harp, as he replied, "Rise up, my love, my fair one, and come away. For lo, the winter is past; the rain is over and gone; the flowers appear on the earth; the time of the singing of birds is come, and the voice of the turtle is heard in our land; the fig tree putteth forth her green figs, and the vines with the tender grape give a good smell. Arise, my love, my fair one, and come away."

Gladly did the soul follow her divine Guide.

> "His robe was white as flakes of snow
> When through the air descending;
> I saw the clouds beneath him melt,
> And rainbows o'er him bending!—

And then a voice — no, not a voice —
A deep and calm revealing
Came through me, like a vesper strain
O'er tranquil waters stealing.

"And ever since that countenance
Is on my pathway shining,
A sun from out a higher sky,
Whose light knows no declining;
All day it falls upon my road,
To keep my feet from straying,
And when at night I lay me down,
I fall asleep while praying."

The mystery of my gaining the Happy Islands, just as I ceased to struggle, was afterwards made plain to me. The great condition of salvation is to be willing to be saved, and to be saved without doing any thing to merit it. God needs no *entreating* to make him willing to restore us fully to our lost holiness, as if it were a work which he was reluctant to undertake. If we would be fully saved, and abide in the peace of God, we must banish all such jealous feelings of him, and maintain a constant assurance that he loves us and desires our highest good. He is not only good, but is goodness itself — he not only loves us, but he is pure, unbounded love itself. This love is always available to the soul. It is coextensive with his being and his presence. It pervades with himself all space. It is the all-surrounding element of the soul. Such a being is not subject to any sudden caprice of passion or feeling. His love is not a transient emotion, changeable as the form of a floating summer cloud, but an unchanging nature. He loves us when we are fearful he does not, and unbelief has forced a barrier between us and his infinite Spirit, and shut us out from the *enjoyment* of his love. It is only a want of affectionate confidence in him that prevents our enjoying him at all times. Nothing can separate the soul from an interior communion with him, and open a chasm between us and the Holy One, but unbelief, a want of that confiding spirit, that loving trust in him, which hath great recompense of reward. This faith was man's original state, and salvation is the reproduction in the soul of that faith in which it was created. It was unbelief that removed man from the paradisiacal state, and blighted and blasted all the fair scene, changing it into the ante-chamber of hell. When the soul comes back from its jealousy of God, and returns to that affectionate confidence it has lost, and maintains an undoubting persuasion of his unchanging and everlasting love through Christ, paradise is repaired, its long-absent God is restored to the spirit, and it enjoys a perpetual and blissful intercourse with his all-pervading presence. Then we can say, —

> "Where'er I am, where'er I move,
> I meet the object of my love."

It is faith that opens the heart, and the infinite Spirit again flows into it, as says Christ, " Behold I stand at the door and knock : if any man hear my voice, and open the door, I will come in unto him, and will sup with him, and he with me." Here is a sensuous image of spiritual delights. To feast with Christ, to recline at the table of God, is not only to be made a partaker of the divine nature, but to share the bliss and unutterable repose of the divine Mind. It is the finite spirit drinking from the fountain of God's own pleasures. This is more than the fabled *ambrosia* and *nectar* of the Greek mythology — it is a peace unknown to the sensual mind, a joy unspeakable. The attitude of Christ before the door of the heart, calling with his voice, and knocking to arouse the slumberer within, indicates a desire on his part to enter. When free will ceases all resistance, and gives way before his infinite love, that yearns over us to do us good, and ends all its inward strugglings to grasp salvation in its own strength, and when the spirit *sinks* into the bosom of the divine love, then God comes into its hidden recess, and fills all its powers, just as, when an artificial embankment gives way, the ocean overflows the land.

When we cease to bolt Christ out as a thief, and invite him in as a friend, he will come in and spread the feast of God, the heavenly manna.

In the Meditations of Guigo, one of the distinguished Christian teachers of the middle age, there seems to be an apprehension of the way in which the soul must reach its supreme good in a state of inward communion with God. He perceived, perhaps, from his own efforts after peace, that we cannot, by struggling, break the fetters of the spirit. In the above-named work, it is said, " The way to God is easy, for a man walks in it by unburdening himself. It would be hard were it necessary for him to take up a load. Throw off then every burden, by denying all else and thyself." (Neander's *History of Christianity and the Church*, vol. iv. p. 413.) How forcibly also does Tauler say to those who pant for deliverance from their inward bondage, " Know that, shouldst thou let thyself be stabbed a thousand times a day, and come to life again; shouldst thou let thyself be strung to a wheel, and eat thorns and stones; with all this thou couldst not overcome sin of thyself. But sink thyself into the deep, unfathomable mercy of God, with a humble, submissive will, under God, and all creatures, and know then that Christ alone would give it thee, out of his great kindness, and free goodness, and love, and compassion."

CHAPTER II.

A DESCRIPTION OF THE HAPPY ISLANDS.

The Number and Names of the Islands. — A Description of them. — Staurosis. — The Altar of Repose. — The Covenant signed. — Full Consecration. — The Land explored — The Inhabitants. — Locality of the primitive Paradise. — Christianity restores Paradise. — First, as a moral State. — Secondly, as an external Condition. — The Elements of the Paradisiacal State. — The Beauties and Harmonies of the outward World. — Fellowship with God. — Communion of holy Souls. — The Inhabitants of the Islands not numerous. — Is it a permanent state? — Bernard of Clairvaux.

AFTER A voyage unnecessarily protracted and difficult, the good land which had been the object of my search was gained. The islands were found to be seven in number, and were called Staurosis, Anapausis, Plerophoria, Euphrosyne, Teleia Agape, Eleutheria, Henotia. In our language they are called Entire Consecration, Rest, Full Assurance of Faith, Fulness of Joy, Perfect Love, Liberty, and Divine Union. They were not situated far from each other, and the passage from one to the other was easy. Below the surface they were united, and constituted but one system. They were arranged at nearly equal distances around Henotia, or Divine Union, which seemed to be the centre of the group. There were also in the distance several smaller isles, that appeared full of beauty, and were far better than the land I had left. But it will be necessary to describe only the seven principal ones. The island on which I had been cast was Staurosis. It was in the form of a cross, as it lay upon the bosom of the deep. It appeared, when seen in the distance, the least lovely of the whole group; yet all who came to the Happy Islands must land here, as it contained the only harbor accessible to ships. As the voyager observes it at a distance it appears somewhat repulsive, but it constitutes the gate to this earthly Paradise. It is surrounded by high and precipitous rocks, and no verdure can be seen. I observed a few solitary, dry trees, looking like the skeleton of what they once were, standing upon the brow of a barren cliff. The top of the island, one would suppose, must be the court of the angel of death, instead of

the palace of life. The summit appeared wholly
inaccessible, but the ascent to it was less difficult
than it seemed, though it is certain no one without aid could ever find the safe path or walk in it.
But the Divine Man who met me on the beach
kindly took me by the hand, and by his aid and
guidance I clambered up the rocks without much
effort. Whenever my foot slipped, and I was in
danger of falling into the abyss below, he caught
me. Sometimes he bore me in his arms as a shepherd would carry a sick lamb. At times I went
forward leaning upon his shoulder. Though the
island was lofty, and apparently so difficult of access, yet when the summit was gained, and the
interior reached, there was spread out before me a
scene of surpassing loveliness. It was full of divine beauty. Never had my eye beheld so delightful a place. Though in the distance it had
appeared bleak and desolate, yet when the summit
was gained, a residence fit for the angels was found.
The soul felt, on reaching this lovely place, like
the traveller who has wandered over the earth,
and at length, escaping from all his perils by sea
and land, comes in sight of the quiet spot that

gave him birth, and the sweet home whose image had followed him in all his roamings. So now I felt that home was gained at last.

My divine Guide directed me at first to a spot in a sequestered vale, where was a large flat rock in shape of an altar, covered with a downy moss, and standing in the midst of flowers. On this I was directed to lie down and rest. I closed my eyes upon all created things, and sunk into a divine repose. It was the state described by the spouse, "I sleep, but my heart waketh." In this divine slumber which steals over the wearied spirit, it ceases from all effort in thinking, all clamorous desires are silenced, and the mind loses itself in the depths of God. Earthly images fade away, and the soul floats sweetly inward from the circumference, becoming tranquilly fixed upon its divine centre. This divine slumber is necessary to the rest of the powers of the soul, and to recruit its energies for the renewed battle of life. The spirit sleeps in God. Perhaps the Psalmist refers to this when he says, "He giveth his beloved sleep." (Ps. cxxvii. 2.) The soul lies becalmed on the ocean of God's presence. Fenelon speaks from the depths of his own inward experience, when he says, in his Pious Thoughts, that, " the presence of God calms the spirit, gives a peaceful slumber and repose, even during the daytime, and in the midst of all our labors." How sweet thus, with the mind free from all disturbing emotions and desires, and all active labored thought, to fall into a divine slumber, as gentle as that of an infant, to hide ourselves, in the secret place of the Most High, from all care and anxiety, and in inward silence to sympathize with the infinite repose of God. There are times after long-continued thought and exertion of our powers in the work of the Master, when the soul needs not ecstatic bliss, but only asks for rest. This holy slumber is not perhaps designed to be a permanent state, but is enjoyed only as the soul needs repose. Then, with its tired energies, it lies down in the ante-chamber of heaven, and sweetly sleeps in the Lord. " There remaineth a rest to the people of God."

While resting upon this altar, there sweetly float out from the soul into the listening ear of a present God the words. " Here, Lord, I give myself away. I present to thee my body, and my whole inward being, a living sacrifice, holy and acceptable in thy sight." No one can explore the Happy Islands until he has deposited his will at the feet of Christ, and delivered over the keeping of it into the hands of the highest Wisdom and Goodness. In reaching a state of complete consecration, we sometimes suppose we must give to our divine Benefactor a list of all our possessions, making them over to him one by one. But there is a shorter method of reaching this desired position. If we give to him our will, we give to him all that our will controls, which is the extent of the divine requirement. Whoever says, "Lo, I come to do thy will, O God," will find in that surrender and self-abandonment the vital germ of a holy disposition and life.

When I arose, my attention was arrested by the mountain side which bounded this sequestered vale. The perpendicular rock, which was like polished marble, rose to a great height. Near the summit this inscription was plainly seen, deeply cut in large gilt letters, and surmounted by a golden cross: " Here I relinquish all, and take God, the infinite and uncreated Good, for my sole portion and inheritance, aiming to enjoy him in all things, and all

things in him. I will seek no good out of him
and separate from him. In return for so great a
treasure, my poor self, with all its powers, shall
be unreservedly his forever. I will love, serve,
and obey him with all my heart, asking no return
but himself." I ascertained from my Guide that
all who contemplated a residence in the Happy
Islands must subscribe this New Covenant. Hence
the mountain side was covered with names, some
of which were familiar to me. There were seen
engraved in the solid rock the names of Anselm of
Canterbury, Bernard of Clairvaux, Raymund Lull,
Thomas à Kempis, Tauler, Ruysbrock, Fenelon,
Madame Guyon, John and Charles Wesley, Mr.
Fletcher and his devoted wife, Elizabeth Rowe,
Hester Ann Rogers, Carvasso, Bramwell, Payson,
Bunyan, Baxter, and innumerable other honored
and sainted names. When it was observed that
these holy men and women had long resided in
this happy region, surely, thought I, "we are not
come unto the mount that might be touched, and
that burned with fire, nor unto blackness, and
darkness, and tempest, but we are come unto
Mount Sion, and unto the city of the living God,

the heavenly Jerusalem, and to an innumerable company of angels, to the general assembly and church of the first born which are written in heaven, and to God the Judge of all, and to the spirits of just men made perfect, and to Jesus the mediator of the new covenant, and to the blood of sprinkling, that speaketh better things than that of Abel." (Heb. xii. 18–24.) With a diamond kept for the purpose, I felt it an unspeakable privilege and honor to record my worthless name beneath all the rest. Falling upon my knees, it was written with the point of the diamond in the rock forever.

Being inwardly refreshed and recovered from all weariness, having renewed my strength, I set myself to acquire a perfect knowledge of these delightful islands, which seemed a fit residence for our first parents in their original innocence. The poets had never in their loftiest imaginings described a more lovely spot than was here actually spread out before me. It was more than the celebrated groves of Daphne, near Antioch, or the valley of Tacoronte, amid the solitudes of Mount Teneriffe, which Humboldt pronounces the most beautiful spot in the world : here was a place

surpassing in divine beauty the celebrated vale of
Tempe, where the eye revels in a scene of loveliness,
and which a Greek writer calls "a festival for the
eyes." I saw fountains glittering in the sun, and
raining pearls; gentle rivulets reflecting from their
silvery surface the heavens above; gravelled walks
lined with flowers, and sometimes passing through
long arbors and arches of blossoming vines; cascades
tumbling down the hill-sides, becoming brooks rolling over golden sands, and meandering through
fertile meadows. Here were flowers that seemed
relics of Paradise, which were never blasted by
wintry frosts. These were not arranged with the
stiff formality of art, but scattered about in rich
profusion on the hills, and plains, and in the vales,
and lining the banks of gently flowing rivers.
There were clusters or miniature forests of all beautiful trees, not inaccessible from matted briers and
thorns, but open and carpeted with green grass,
making natural bowers, inviting the soul to repose
and divine contemplation. Fruits of every kind and
of richest taste every where met the eye, urging man
to leave the feast of blood, on which depravity has
revelled, and come back to the primitive food of

Eden. Vines laden with their tempting clusters climbed the trees and clothed the naked rocks with verdure. Here were lakes sleeping in their quiet beauty among the hills, on which the moonbeams sweetly reposed at night, and which were dotted with verdant isles. The air was soft and balmy, pure as the celestial ether, and perfumed like the breezes of Arabia Felix, the land of frankincense, spices, and myrrh. It diffused a delightful tranquillity through the whole system. The sun did not smite by day, nor the moon by night. " Stern winter smiles on that auspicious clime." Here were birds of the richest plumage and sweetest song, who flew from branch to branch unalarmed at the approach of man, delighting to receive their food from the hands of children. The lark filled the grove with her melody, and the swan floated upon the lake a buoyant and beautiful thing, fashioned by the Creator to adorn the waste of waters. The animals were tame as they once were in Eden, and dwelt in mutual peace and love. The deer came forth from the forest to meet and welcome the approach of man. The vision of the prophet seemed to be realized — " The wolf shall dwell with the lamb, and the leopard shall lie down with the kid; and they shall not hurt nor destroy in all my holy mountain." In all this scene of beauty which was spread before the eye of sense, faith saw God. It was this that made it appear so lovely to the purified soul. Outward nature was not viewed as something existing separate from him. These things had their root in the Divine Life itself. He did not create them and then leave them, but creates them every moment out of himself. In the Happy Isles the soul can say with the poet Moore, —

> "Thou art, O God, the life and light
> Of all this wondrous world we see;
> Its glow by day, its smile by night,
> Are but reflections caught from thee.
> Where'er we turn thy glories shine,
> And all things fair and bright are thine."

The inhabitants of the Happy Islands bore a striking resemblance to the lovely being whom I had first met. They were clothed in flowing robes white as the newly-fallen snow, a fine linen, soft as silk. Here they dwelt in innocence and love, each rejoicing in the happiness of others as much as in his own, and united to each other by the strongest possible bond — the common love of God. Their countenance was radiant with divine peace, which moulded the features into a form which became its outward and permanent expression. There was a divine cheerfulness which pervaded this redeemed society. They walked in holy communion with God, and in an endearing fellowship with each other. Here was a fulfilment of the promise, "All thy people shall be righteous." They were a royal priesthood, a holy generation, a peculiar people. Their prayers went up at all times from a thousand shady bowers, or vine-clad cottages. The hills were vocal with praise. Here no crime was ever committed, no unhallowed thought entered, no vulgar or profane expression polluted the atmosphere. No brawls and drunken revellings broke the silence of midnight. In a word, here Christ lived and reigned as the Restorer of Paradise. In this spot he began to open the golden gates of a celestial day, and to pour the "living light of heaven" upon the moral gloom of a sin-ruined world. Here Christianity entered upon the last stadium of its earthly progress, and exhibited the commencement of its millennial development.

There had once been in the world a spot called Paradise, situated somewhere in the territory called Eden. (Gen. ii. 8, 9.) Where it was has faded from human recollection. The mind of the race has longed to find it, and identify the place where dwelt the primitive innocence. With little to guide the search but imagination, it has been located in various places — in the third heaven, in the orb of the moon, in the middle region of the air, above the earth and under the earth, in a realm hidden from the knowledge of men, in the place possessed at present by the Caspian Sea, in the north of Europe, especially in Prussia. Men have looked for it in Asia, Africa, Europe, and America; on the banks of the Danube, and the Ganges, in the Isle of Ceylon, and in Mesopotamia; some have found it, as they supposed, near the city of Damascus, and others among the " blameless Ethiopians," near the Mountains of the Moon. That happy and holy place, where man dwelt in innocence and love. and walked with God in unsullied bliss, has long ago disappeared from the world. Its existence is still faintly attested in the heathen world, by the prevalent tradition of a golden age, when God dwelt with men, and men in peace with each other. This fond remembrance lingers in the heart of humanity like the summer's twilight after the sun has sunk behind the western hills. The restless soul loves to revel in this traditionary twilight, and inwardly yearns to hail again the rising sun. It was sin that blotted out Paradise from the earth. There is profound truth in the poetry of Milton, that when our first parents sinned, " Earth felt the wound, and nature sighed through all her works." Sin entered the soul, and Paradise vanished from the map of the mind. For it was not so much a physical change in the outward world, as a change in the moral standing-ground from which nature was viewed, and in the spiritual medium through which the soul gazes upon the divine arrangements of the material universe.*

---

* Professor Schleiden has truly remarked that the earth in itself is neither fair nor foul, but all our pleasure in beholding it is from the human spirit, which has received from God the gift to feel beauty in all that surrounds us. (*Poetry of the Vegetable World*, p. 33.) It is the condition of the powers of our souls which lends to earth all its charms. It is fair to suppose that brutes discern nothing of the kind in the things around them.

Paradise was expunged by sin from the map of the human spirit, and will be restored when man is raised by Christ and Christianity to his original moral position, and the soul again reflects the heavenly things, just as the placid lake at night mirrors from its glassy surface the celestial orbs. Paradise must be sought within, and will be found in that spirit which makes a prison a palace, and December as pleasant as May.

It is the mission of Christianity to restore to earth its lost Paradise. It has pleased God that there should ever be a harmony and correspondence between man's moral character and his external condition. When sin entered into the world, Paradise became an unsuitable residence for the race, as it did not correspond to his character, and was not suited to be the theatre of the discipline of a race of sinners. But it is not forever lost to the world. It shall be restored by Christ. This has ever been the expectation of the world. The heathen while they cast a longing look back to the golden age which had fled, looked forward with hope to its return. The sentiment prevailed extensively in the Gentile world, just before the advent of the Messiah, that the glad era of its restoration was about to dawn upon the world. The Jews connected the reappearance of the paradisiacal state with the coming of the Christ. No one can fail to observe this who reads the glowing descriptions of the Messianic age in the Hebrew prophets. All nature would sympathize with the coming of the great Restorer. The wilderness and the solitary place should be glad, and the desert should rejoice and blossom as the rose. He would comfort Zion and all her waste places, and make her wilderness like Eden, and her desert like the garden of the Lord. There should be joy and gladness therein, thanksgiving and the voice of melody. Springs would break forth in the sandy plains. The adornments and excellences that still remain in the sin-blasted earth were to be greatly increased. The light of the moon would be as the light of the sun, and the light of the sun sevenfold, as the light of seven days, in the day when the Lord should bind up the breach of his people, and heal the stroke of their wound. The discords which had followed the fall, and been introduced by the disturbing influence of sin, were to subside into divine harmony. The wolf would dwell with the lamb, and the leopard would lie down with the kid, and the calf and the young lion and the fatling together, and a little child should lead them. Men should bruise their swords into ploughshares and their spears into pruning hooks ; nation should not lift up sword against nation, neither should they learn war any more. There shall be a substantial fulfilment of these prophetic announcements, for not one word that proceedeth out of the mouth of the Lord shall fall to the ground. This restoration of nature in the Messianic times, by the Jewish prophets, may be thought only emblematic of the higher moral and intellectual recovery of the race by earth's living Redeemer. It is admitted that this is symbolical of that new moral creation which was to go forth from Christ and Christianity; and yet we aver that there is an objective truth underlying these glowing predictions. The reëstablishment of the original harmony between the natural and moral world is one of the aims of the redemptive scheme. One of the elements of the paradisiacal state is found in the beauties and harmonies of outward nature. Christianity shall restore all this to the world in two ways, one of them subjective, and the other objective. Christ shall heal earth's dreadful wound, and open also in the souls of men an inward sense for the appreciation and enjoyment of the beauties of nature already existing. Before the soul of man can fully perceive and enjoy the beauty of the outward world already existing, it must be placed in the proper moral attitude while he views it. This is the truth at bottom in the words of Christ, (Matt. v. 5,) " Blessed are the meek, for they shall inherit the earth." With the first beginnings of the soul's restoration the appearance of outward nature is changed. No sooner does the love of God for his own sake, as the most perfect being, possessing infinite moral beauty, find a place in the human soul, than nature is felt to possess new charms, and earth becomes like Bunyan's Delectable Mountains or Land of Beulah. How often is the remark made by such a person that all things seem to be new ! The new moral creation within is reflected upon things without, and there appear to be new heavens and a new earth, because they are beheld through the medium of new feelings and are seen from a different stand-point. The harmony of the restored moral nature with the outward world deepens with the progress of the redeemed spirit in holiness. It sees in the beautiful moving forms of earth what Jerome calls *radios Deitatis*, radiations of the Deity, and emanations of the beauty of the Lord. The pure in heart see all things to be full of God, and the whole material universe is viewed, in a certain sense, as *Deum explicatum*, the unfoldings or manifestations of God. The successive seasons, with the beauties and harmonies belonging to each, are exhibitions of the Deity.

> "These, as they change, almighty Father, these
> Are but the *varied* God. The rolling year
> Is full of thee."

The earth, though sympathizing with the moral disorders of mankind, still exhibits traces of its original perfection, some lingering marks of its paradisiacal order and bloom. Enough of its original beauty gleams through its present disorder to convince us that it was not made to be the abode of sin, and of beings made miserable by sin. Those who complain of the outward world as an unsuitable residence for man, will find the seat of their misery within their own hearts. Montgomery, who had a soul fitted to appreciate the beauties of nature, remarks, that " the earth, arrayed in verdure, adorned with flowers, diversified with hill and dale, forest and glade, fountains and running streams, engirdled with the ocean, over-canopied with heaven, — this earth, so smiling and fruitful, so commodious and magnificent, is altogether worthy of its Maker, and not only a fit habitation for man created in the image of God, but a place which angels might delight to visit on embassies of love." (*Lectures on Poetry*, p. 52.) It is only the pure in heart who can fully enjoy so fair a world as even this. Sin draws a veil over the beautiful creations of the divine hand. But the earth is full of divine radiance, and the relics of its original adornment. The redeemed spirit, adjusted in harmony with all that is divine, finds them on every hand. Such a soul —

> "makes music with the common strings
> With which the world is strung, and makes the dumb
> Earth utter heavenly harmony."

This is a subjective restoration of the earth. It is like the opening of the eyes of the blind to behold beauties which had ever been invisible. But there shall be an objective restoration of the earth. This is the truth underlying that obscure prophecy in Rom. viii. 19–21: "For the earnest expectation of the creation waiteth for the manifestation of the sons of God. For the creation was made subject to vanity, not willingly, but by reason of Him who hath subjected the same in hope; because the creation itself also shall be delivered from the bondage of corruption into the glorious liberty of the children of God." A restored nature has ever kept even pace with the progress of human redemption; in fact, it is a part of redemption. In whatever nation there is the most of Christianity, we find there external nature approaches the nearest to the original Paradise. Look at England or America in their heathen state, and those same countries now as constituting a part of the domain of Christianity. It is the realization of the vision of the prophet." In the wilderness shall waters break out, and streams in the desert. And the parched ground shall become a pool, and the thirsty land springs of water. In the habitation of dragons, where each lay, shall be

grass, with reeds and rushes." (Isa. xxxv. 6, 7.)
See this principle illustrated in Germany as it was
in the age of Tacitus, and Germany now. In Ire-
land the traveller can tell a Protestant from a
Catholic county by the appearance of the outward
world. One has told me that if he were set down
blindfolded any where, he could tell, when the ban-
dage was removed, whether he was in a Protestant
or Catholic region. Why this? It is because the
restoration of nature keeps even pace with the
onward march of Christ's redemptive work, and
just in proportion as the intellectual and moral
image of God is restored to the soul, will Paradise begin to bloom without. The miracles of
Christ, among other and higher aims, have demonstrated that nature is passive in his hands, and
that her laws yield at once to the fiat of a present
God. And if Christianity has done so much for
the outward world, notwithstanding its imperfect
triumphs even in Christian lands, what would it
accomplish in a country where it has fully penetrated and appropriated the mind of the people,
and love has become the ruling element of society?
In the Happy Islands such was the case. Conse-

quently the outward world was restored to its original beauty and harmony.

Another element of the moral state we call Paradise was a living fellowship with God. Without this there could have been no Paradise, however beautiful and pleasant might have been the place where man lived. Adam walked with God in unbroken communion of spirit.

> "Not all the harps above
>   Can make a happy place,
> If God his residence remove,
>   Or but conceal his face.
>
> Nor earth, nor all the sky,
>   Can one delight afford,
> Nor yield one drop of real joy,
>   Without thy presence, Lord.
>
> "Thou art the sea of love,
>   Where all my pleasures roll,
> The circle where my passions move,
>   And centre of my soul."

This heavenly communion, this divine society, was broken up by sin. The soul was sundered from God, and estranged from him. Through the disjunctive agency of sin, Adam fled from God, and all the race in him. There sprang up in his soul

a sense of distance between him and the Holy
One. The mutual attraction founded upon a harmony and affinity of nature ceased to draw the
infinite and finite spirits together. But what we lost
in Adam the redeemed soul has gained in Christ.
Christianity brings the sanctified spirit, when the
separating veil is rent away, and the middle wall of
partition removed, and faith's interior eye opened,
into a nearer and closer relation to God, and union
with him, than was ever seen in Paradise. God
in human form is not now, as then, a mere appearance, but an objective reality, a living and
eternal truth. By the assumption of human nature,
God is joined to man in a nearer and diviner fellowship than in Eden. Paradise had no incarnation. This was the mystery, as St. Paul declares,
that was hid from ages, until Heaven broke the
seals in Bethlehem, and the greatest truth in the
universe flashed upon the world, and God was manifest in the flesh. But did not Adam see God,
and hear his voice, amid the blissful groves of Paradise? It is certain that he did; and does not
Christ say, " Blessed are the pure in heart, for they
shall see God"? Holiness in the spirit restores

God again to human consciousness, and reveals him every where. He *manifests* himself to the redeemed heart. He has written it in the New Covenant, and it is a part of the divine compact with us, " I will dwell in them, and walk in them, and I will be their God, and they shall be my people." The baptism of the Holy Ghost on the day of Pentecost fully restored to the Christian mind that original fellowship with God in which man was created. " If we walk in the light as he [Christ] is in the light, we have fellowship one with another, [God with us, and we with him,] and the blood of Jesus Christ, his Son, cleanseth us from all sin." Behold, then, the prime element of the paradisiacal state completely brought back to earth by Christ. The pure in heart will not search long nor wander far to find an every-where present God.

> "No sun arose — I saw no moon
>   Go paling through the air;
> God's glorious presence, like a sun,
>   Was here — was every where;
> It brooded o'er the flowering plains,
>   On all the hills it glowed;
> If here I looked, or there I looked,
>   I saw the face of God."

Another element of Paradise, which was found restored in the Happy Islands, was the union of the race in peace and love. The only disjunctive agency that ever separated men from God and from each other was here removed. The disturbing influence of sin being taken away, souls spontaneously united in the bonds of an unbroken fellowship. Every one loved his neighbor as himself. Each lived for the good of the whole. In the very act of giving all to God, selfishness, the root of all social evils, had been destroyed. The souls of the inhabitants were first joined to the Lord, and became one spirit with him; and as the rays of a circle all meet in the centre, so here all were made one in Christ. All holy beings in the universe have fellowship and communion in God. The ancient Persian Magi and Chaldeans supposed there was a certain "vital sympathy" between the superior and lower orders of being. So in this delightful region, the soul enjoyed a closer sympathy with the celestial world than was enjoyed any where else. Their hearts beat in unison with the heavenly state. They bowed their knees before the Father of our Lord Jesus Christ, of whom the

whole family in heaven and earth is named. (Eph.
iii. 14, 15.) One common principle of life went
forth from Christ to animate the whole. Would
you see Paradise restored, so far as it was made
up of a union of soul to soul around Christ, the
centre, look at the fellowship of genuine Christian
hearts.

> "Blest are the sons of peace,
>   Whose hearts and hopes are one;
> Whose kind designs to serve and please
>   Through all their actions run.
>
> Thus on the heavenly hills,
>   The saints are blest above,
> Where joy like morning dew distils,
>   And all the air is love."

Christianity has created a stronger love for man
than Paradise would have ever known. Eden never
heard the prayer of a dying Christ, amid the ago-
nies of his atoning death struggle, saying, " Father,
forgive; they know not what they do." This was
not merely the ejaculation of the dying Messiah, that
was to cease forever in the world, like an echo
dying away among the hills. It was an emanation
or outgrowth from that divine life he came to deposit in humanity. It reappeared in Stephen, pray-

ing for his murderers; in Paul, declaring that he
would willingly be made an expiatory victim, if by
so doing he could save his countrymen; and in
Howard journeying from country to country to re-
lieve human misery.

One thing in regard to the inhabitants of the
Happy Islands strikes the visitor with much force.
They are not so numerous as he would suppose
they would be. Compared with what the country
would sustain, the population is small. This seems
almost unaccountable. Many believe in their existence, and seem resolved some time to emigrate
to them. But comparatively few ever find them,
because the time for commencing the voyage is
always placed in the future. The inhabitants are
intensely desirous that all should come and share
their blessedness; and one of their delightful labors
is to keep watch from the mountain top for any
one who may be struggling with the waves to gain
the land, in order that they may hasten to his
aid. Though the population was not numerous,
yet it is a matter of joy that it is steadily increasing, and the day is not very distant when it will
amount to many millions.

This restored Paradise was what my soul had long inwardly craved. Here the needs of my nature found satisfaction and rest. Yet during the first weeks of my stay, a fear would insinuate itself into the heart, lest I should be prevailed upon by some influence to go back to the country which had been left. This was sometimes, though not often, the case. Persons occasionally left the islands, intending to return after a brief visit to their native land, but were never seen here again. Sometimes I was fearful lest I should be foolish enough to leave. I suggested this anxiety to a venerable man, who wore a look of heavenly benignity, and who had resided here for a long period. His name was Bernard. I told him there was nothing from which my soul shrunk with greater horror than from the thought of losing this blissful communion with God in the centre of my soul, which Adam enjoyed in Paradise, and which had been restored to the pure in heart, who dwelt in the Happy Islands. I could not endure the idea of again being put back upon the ordinary Christian position, where the soul, instead of this pure spirituality, was filled with earthy and sensuous images, and God was well nigh excluded. The venerable saint informed me, that when any temptation arose from any source to leave the islands, I should, at once, whatever might be my employment at the time, leave all, and walk to the rock where I had written my name, and mark it still deeper with the point of the diamond. He had done this until his name was engraved so deep that neither the storms of heaven nor the changes of time could efface it; and for many years he had felt neither desire nor fear that he should return to his native land. The misery and inexpressible emptiness of a soul that starts to return constitutes a force to draw the soul back.

He also informed me that after one had visited all the islands, and resided here for some time, the powerful law of habit would have time to exert its influence; habits of holy living would be formed; our *nature* would become thoroughly changed; the depraved bent of the will reversed, and the will would become fixed in the direction of God and heaven; the soul would pass into a state of comparative, though not absolute immutability. The soul then becomes like a gentle stream that flows

on day and night, reflecting the heavens above.
The great object of a probationary state is the
formation of fixed habits of holiness. When the
will of God, expressing itself in the laws of our
mental nature, shall say, "Let him that is holy be
holy still," we have attained the great end of existence here, and are prepared in a higher sphere
of life to commence the race of endless progression
in knowledge, purity, and love.

CHAPTER III.

THE SUPREME GOOD SOUGHT AND FOUND.

THE HAPPY region, in which I had come to reside, seemed every way fitted to be the blissful abode of a soul made in the image of God. The beauty of the outward world surpassed any thing I had ever seen in any part of the world, and seemed truly divine. A susceptibility of the emotion of the beautiful, when the soul is in the presence of the skilful creations of the divine hand, is one of the original powers of our nature, and the beneficent Creator has made the most ample provision for its gratification. There is no part of the world, not even a burning desert, nor the region around the throne of everlasting winter, where the objects of the creative Love do not appear radiant with the dimmed rays of celestial beauty, and we are constrained to say, "God is even here!" But created earthly beauty does not fully satisfy the soul. It is only the type of those more solid realities which eternity shall disclose, and which adorn the heavenly plains. The feeling grows with that upon which it feeds, and soon transcends the finite, the transient, the earthly, and demands for its rest the uncreated and the infinite. This was suggested to me in the Happy Islands, as I was passing a retired place, where, in a most delightful spot, was a bower, within which I heard the soft voice of Mrs. Elizabeth Rowe conversing with God. These words I distinctly caught: "I love my friends; my vital breath and the light of heaven are dear to me; but should I say, I love my God as I love these, I should belie the sacred flame which aspires to infinity. 'Tis thee, abstractedly thee, O uncreated Beauty, that I love; in thee my wishes all terminate; in thee, as in their blissful centre, all my desires meet, and there they must be eternally fixed; it is thou alone must constitute my everlasting happiness."

No tongue can describe the refined pleasure of the soul, which, released from the bondage of sense, rises to the contemplation of the infinite beauty of the divine character. It is a bliss no sensual mind can taste, and places the holy soul on the imperfectly defined boundary line between earth and heaven. In this spiritual position earth projects into heaven, like a promontory into the ocean, or a mountain summit above the clouds and earthy vapors. Such a one will ever pray, "Let the beauty of the Lord our God be upon us." (Ps. xc. 17.) Also, with David, the soul can say, "One thing have I desired of the Lord, that will I seek after; that I may dwell in the house of the Lord all the days of my life, to behold the beauty of the Lord." (Ps. xxvii. 4.) Isaiah represents the felicity of the celestial state as consisting in part of the gratification of this refined emotion.

"Thine eyes shall see the King in his beauty." (Isa. xxxiii. 17.)

In the Happy Islands the soul finds itself possessed of an ineffable longing for a sweeter consciousness of God; a clearer inward sense of the divine presence. Says Richard Watson in a letter to a friend, "Rest not a moment without the *felt* presence of your God." From the time I started for this blissful region, I was consumed with a deathless inward craving for God. Long had I inquired of the philosophers of the old world what constitutes the supreme good, the *summum bonum* — a good completely satisfying all the desires of the heart. From the time of Socrates, philosophy had turned its inquiries in that direction, and had diligently searched for it, in order that the human spirit might reach a position of perfect mental tranquillity and profound satisfaction. But philosophy proved a false light, whose guidance only served to bewilder. It created aspirations which it could not conduct to their proper object; it excited a thirst it had no power to allay. According to Varro, as quoted by St. Augustine, the philosophers entertained *two hundred and eighty-eight* different opinions upon what constitutes the supreme good. Some placed it in one thing, some in another. But all were wrong, for they looked for it among finite things, and stopped short of the uncreated and infinite One. Leaving philosophy, with its twilight flashes of truth, for the unerring guidance of revelation, I soon learned that the conscious possession of God, the infinite and eternal Good, from whom all other good proceeds, was the highest bliss, the supreme and all-satisfying felicity of a human soul. The universe itself, empty of him, would be a boundless desolation, a dreary solitude. All things without God are as nothing to the soul; and in the possession of him, with nothing else, we have all. How often, in the midst of earthly delights, and in the possession of the creatures of God, we feel inwardly desolate and unhappy, we know not why! Though our condition may be the object of desire or envy to others, yet something is lacking to fill the measure of our satisfaction, and give repose to our restless spirits. Happy the man who knows at such times what his nature demands, and says, " I will arise and go to my Father." The soul was made for the enjoyment of God, and must return to him for rest. Blessed is the man whose desires soar beyond all created good, that rise from the shadow to grasp the substance.

An inward longing of the soul after God has been characteristic of the experience of good men in all ages. The human spirit sundered from its Source, and cut off from the enjoyment of its supreme good, is like the magnetic needle when forcibly drawn aside from its true polar direction. It restlessly vibrates back and forth until it settles down in its natural position, where alone it can become quiet. Job stands forth as the representative of our common humanity, when he says, "O that I knew where I might find him! Behold I go forward, but he is not there; and backward, but I cannot perceive him; on the left hand, where he doth work, but I cannot behold him; he hideth himself on the right hand, that I cannot see him." (Job xxiii. 3, 8, 9.) David often expresses this pious breathing of the soul after God. "As the hart panteth [or brayeth, referring to the complaining moan which that animal makes] after the water brooks, so panteth my soul after thee, O

God." (Ps. xlii. 1, 2.) In another place he exclaims, "O God, thou art my God; early will I seek thee: my soul thirsteth for thee, my flesh longeth for thee, in a dry and thirsty land, where no water is." (Ps. lxiii. 1.) As the traveller across a burning desert, who has been days without water, pants for a cooling fountain, so the spirit of man yearns for God. When God is absent from our consciousness, in our emptiness and dissatisfaction, we ask, with the spouse, "Saw ye him whom my soul loveth?" In such a spiritual orphanage, the heart from its inmost centre prays, "Come, Lord Jesus, come quickly."

All men long for God, or at least for that which he alone can supply — the infinite and all-satisfying good. St. Paul, who had a profound knowledge of the workings of the human spirit, in his oration before the Areopagus at Athens, represents the heathen mind, while in the unenlightened midnight of nature, as feeling after God, like a blind man groping along the wall. (Acts xvii. 27.) In this way Plato searched for the hidden God, and with some success, for the heart of God is touched with the sincere longings of even pagan minds. He listens to the secret sighs of such souls, and answers their deep yearnings by imperfect manifestations of himself to their consciousness. Plato in the Timæus says, " To discover the Creator and Father of this universe, as well as his work, is indeed difficult; and when discovered, it is impossible to reveal him to mankind." But Christianity, in the person of Paul, came to Athens to reveal the Unknown to the Grecian philosophy. Under her light the Deity is no longer the " *Great Unrevealed* " of Basilides, nor the unexplored *Abyss* of the Gnostic Valentine, nor the cold, indifferent, iron-hearted *Animus Mundi*, or Soul of the World, of the Stoics, but a God of eternal love, who is not far from every one of us, and who delights to manifest himself to all souls who long for his presence.

In the Christian heart the desire for God is supreme, and absorbs every other desire. It is a powerfully attractive force, drawing the soul from the noisy world to the silence and solitude of the closet, and onward in its course to heaven. The more of holiness we attain, the more forcibly this divine gravitation of the soul towards its centre is felt. In my childhood I read in the Arabian Nights of a mountain of loadstone. Ships at a great distance felt its influence; but at first their approach to it was scarcely perceptible. There was only a very slight deviation from their course, which excited but little apprehension. But the attraction gradually became stronger, until by its invisible influence the vessel was impelled onward with increased velocity. At last it drew all the nails and iron-work to itself, and the ship fell to pieces. Thus it is with the soul. In the commencement of its moral recovery, when it first feels the love of Christ, it is drawn towards him it loves. Absence from him begins to be viewed as the most dreaded calamity, and separation from him becomes our ideal of hell. At length, united to him by a perfect sympathy of character, it can no longer be kept from him it loves. It flies to his presence and eternal embrace, and the body is dissolved. The tendency of the holy soul towards God in its desires constitutes unceasing prayer. (1 Thess. v. 17.) This sighing of the spirit after communion and union with the Holy One, when yielded to and properly directed, will draw the soul into an all-satisfying fellowship with the God of love. He gives it by the Holy Spirit in order to satisfy it. As the soul approaches him, he will not retire from it, but will fly to embrace the returning wanderer. The soul that hungers and thirsts after righteousness *is* already blessed, and *shall be* filled.

Raymond Lull (born *anno* 1236, in the Island of Majorca) speaks in harmony with the feelings of every genuinely Christian heart, when he declares, " The spirit longs after nothing as it does after God. No gold is worth so much as a sigh of holy longing. The more of this longing one has, the more of life he has. The want of this longing is death. Have this longing and thou shalt live. He is not poor who possesses this; unhappy the man who lives without it." That ardent craving of the soul after God which cannot be satisfied with his gifts, but demands the infinite Giver, is nowhere, out of the Psalms of David, more forcibly expressed than in the hymns of Charles Wesley. His sacred poetry gushes out from the hidden depths of a profound Christian experience.

"Me with that restless thirst inspire,
That sacred, infinite desire,
　And feast my hungry heart;
Less than thyself cannot suffice;
My soul for all thy fulness cries,
　For all thou hast and art."

"Ever fainting with desire,
　For thee, O Christ, I call;
Thee I restlessly require;
　I want my God, my all."

"Give me thyself, from every boast,
　From every wish set free;
Let all I am in thee be lost,
　But give thyself to me.

Thy gifts, alas! cannot suffice,
　Unless thyself be given;
Thy presence makes my Paradise,
　And where thou art is heaven."

In his eagerness to rise to the enjoyment of
that only bliss for which the soul was made, his
soul "swells to compass" God, and pants to live
and move in its native divine element.

"If now thine influence I feel,
　If now in thee begin to live,
Still to my heart thyself reveal;
　Give me thyself, forever give;
A point my good, a drop my store,
Eager I ask, I pant for more.

> Eager for thee I ask and pant,
>   So strong the principle divine
> Carries me out in sweet constraint
>   Till all my hallowed soul is thine;
> Plunged in the Godhead's deepest sea,
>   And lost in his immensity."

In the Happy Islands this intense thirst of the spirit for God would not suffer us to rest until we had found the infinite Good, and had so appropriated him that we could say, God is ours. The language of the heart was, " Whom have we in heaven but thee? and there is none upon earth we desire beside thee. My flesh and my heart faileth, but God is the strength of my heart and my portion forever." (Ps. lxxiii. 25, 26.) The soul, though subject to finite limitations, was made for the enjoyment of the infinite, and can be content with nothing less. Its unfolding powers must lay hold of its inheritance, or be wretched. As confined flowers instinctively seek the sun, and stretch themselves to meet his embrace, so our souls were drawn out after God. Paradise itself, with all its outward adornments, could not fill the abyss of the heart. It did not satisfy to see him in the beautiful creations of his hand, to recognize

him in the sun rejoicing as a giant to run a race,
or in the moon walking in brightness, or in the
worlds flaming in the infinite spaces above our
heads, or in the dewdrop and the flower. We had
sought and found him in all these. We had seen
him marching at the head of the centuries in human history, controlling and directing all events
and revolutions to the advancement of the redemptive work; but still our flesh and heart cried out
for the living God. He was still too far from the
soul. This distance must be annihilated, or we
cannot attain to perfect tranquillity. We must
grasp the God we seek. We must not only see
him every where without, but find him within.
It is not enough to realize that all things are full
of God, unless he fills our hearts. With a sweet
restlessness I wandered about, inquiring of every
thing I saw, "Where is God, my Maker, who
giveth songs in the night?" It was natural that I
should ask the inhabitants of the islands where I
could so find God as to satisfy the inward craving
of my nature. I recollected to have read in Plutarch, that he did not deem it unreasonable that
a good man should hold converse with the Deity.

He says, in the Life of Numa, that "there were many who were thought to have attained to superior felicity, and to be beloved in an extraordinary manner by the Divinity. And, indeed, it is reasonable enough to suppose that the Deity would not place his affections upon horses or birds, but rather upon human beings eminently distinguished for virtue; and that he neither disdains nor dislikes to hold communion with a man of wisdom and piety." Thus speaks this eminent pagan philosopher. And surely it would be most unreasonable to suppose that the redeemed soul, the noblest work of God, should be cut off from all intercourse with him; that he should sustain by his presence every material thing, and yet would not be consciously present in the human spirit. But who could tell me where to find God. Plutarch could not, for it transcended the power of mere philosophy. I sought that devout and unworldly man, Thomas à Kempis, and asked him, "Where is God, my Maker, who giveth songs in the night?" His words were like a ray of light in a dungeon, and fell upon my soul with the force of a new revelation. as he replied, "My son, if thou withdrawest thy attention from outward things, and keepest it fixed upon what passeth within, thou wilt soon perceive the coming of the kingdom of God, for the kingdom of God is that peace and joy in the Holy Ghost, which cannot be received by sensual and worldly men. All the glory and beauty of Christ are manifested within, and there he delights to dwell; his visits there are frequent, his condescension amazing, his conversation sweet, and the peace that he brings passeth all understanding." (*Imitation of Christ*, p. 137.) Thus my search for God was turned in the proper direction. We are not to look outward, but into the depths of our interior being. We cannot fully find him in the sensible world. It is not by wandering outward through space that we find him fully, but by leaving the realm of sense, and by an introversion of mind, we must retire into the hidden recess of the spirit.

Madam Guyon, in her autobiography, informs us how she was first led to that profound inward experience of God which she attained. She tells us that she restlessly wandered about in search of Him who was infinitely near to her, until one day a pious Franciscan was providentially brought into her society, to whom she related her strivings after God and her want of success. He replied, " It is, madam, because you seek without what you have within. Accustom yourself to seek God in your heart, and you will find him." These words made an indelible impression upon her heart. They seemed to come as from the lips of God. In reference to her past want of success in attaining a satisfying communion with an inwardly present Deity, she exclaims, " Alas! I sought thee where thou wast not. It was for want of understanding these words of thy gospel, 'The kingdom of God cometh not with observation, neither shall they say, Lo here, or, Lo there; for the kingdom of God is within you.'"

Fenelon, whose seraphic love introduced him into the familiar society of the Deity, and who, like Enoch, walked with God, informs us how he sought for him in his works, but could not find him except in the interior of his heart. He says to the Deity, " Thou art (and I am enraptured with the thought) continually at work in the very centre of my being; invisibly thou workest there, as a laborer digging mines in the bowels of the earth; thou dost all, and the world perceives thee not; it attributes nothing to thee. I myself was once wandering astray in vain attempts to find thee, at a great distance from me; I was drawing together all the wonders of nature, that I might then form to myself some image of thy greatness; I was going to inquire after thee of thy creatures; and I never thought of finding thee in the centre of my heart, where thou never ceasest to dwell. No, my God, we need not dig into the heart of the earth, nor pass beyond the seas; we need not, as thy holy oracles tell us, fly up into the heavens to find thee. Thou art nearer to us than we are to ourselves." (*Pious Thoughts*, pp. 40, 41.) In another place, he remarks, "To bid men seek thee in their own hearts, is to propose to them to seek thee at a much greater distance than the most unknown parts of the earth. What is there more unknown and more remote to the greatest part of men, vain and thoughtless, than the bottom of their own hearts? Do they know what it is ever to enter into themselves? Have they ever tried to find the way? Can they so much as imagine what that interior sanctuary is, that impenetrable centre of the soul, where thou desirest to be adored in spirit and in truth? They are continually out of themselves among the objects of their ambition or amusement. * * * As for me, O my Creator, with my eyes shut to all external objects, which are but vanity and vexation of spirit, I will find, in the most secret recess of my heart, an intimate familiarity with thee, by Jesus Christ thy Son." (*Pious Thoughts*, pp. 43, 45.) If we will find God, we must learn to withdraw our minds from every thing which is not God; we must in abstraction from external things retire into the recesses of our spiritual being. Men are not accustomed to this. They know as little of their inward state as most travellers do of the interior chambers of the pyramid of Cheops, on the banks of the Nile, in whose inner solitude dwells the unilluminated darkness of centuries, and dust, which the passing ages have never stirred. He who knows God, not merely as the God of nature, ordering all the movements of the material universe, and who is the secret spring and cause of all its phenomena, nor as the God of history and providence, nor merely as an infinitely perfect Being, intellectually apprehended, but as a

God dwelling in us as in the *penetralia* of a temple
has found the beginnings of eternal life. This is
the fulfilment of the promise of Christ. " If any
man love me, he will keep my commandments;
and my Father will love him, and we will come
unto him and make our abode with him." The
indwelling of God in the soul is the great mystery
of the gospel.

Mr. Baxter seems to have had a clear conception
of the privilege of the purified soul in enjoying the
inward presence of God. According to him the
more holy a person becomes, the nearer and sweeter
is his fellowship with God. His language is, " When
man's heart had nothing in it to grieve the Spirit
it was the delightful habitation of his Maker. God
did not quit his residence there till man expelled
him by unworthy provocations. There was no shyness or reserve till the heart grew sinful, and too
loathsome a dungeon for God to delight in. And
was this soul reduced to its former innocency, God
would quickly return to his former habitation; yea,
so far as it is renewed and repaired by the Spirit,
and purged from its lusts and beautified by his
image, the Lord will yet acknowledge it as his

own, Christ will manifest himself unto it, and the Spirit will take it for his temple and residence. So far as the heart is qualified for conversing with God, so far it usually enjoys him." (*Baxter's Saints' Everlasting Rest*, p. 258.) The proper residence of the soul is in God, and the proper abode of God is in the soul. Every living thing has its native element and place of abode, adapted to its nature and powers. Some occupy the ocean, in whose dark caverns they revel in bliss; some find a happy abode amid the frozen snows of the north; others on the burning sands of the equatorial regions. But every thing God has made has its appropriate *habitat*, out of which locality it cannot be fully blest. The habitation of a human soul is an all-pervading Deity, " whose presence bright all space doth occupy." As says the Psalmist, " O Lord, thou hast been our dwelling place in all generations." Holy love is the unitive principle which restores the soul to its native home. " He that dwelleth in love dwelleth in God, and God in him." (1 John iv. 16.)

It was the remark of that illustrious Christian philosopher, Dr. Neander, of Berlin, that one pe-

culiar characteristic for which the German race
has ever been distinguished is their profound sense
of the religious element seated in the inmost
depths of the human soul, their readiness to be
impelled by the discordant strifes of the external
world, and unfruitful human ordinances, to seek
and find God in the deep recesses of their own
hearts, and to experience a hidden life in God,
springing forth in opposition to barren conceptions
of the abstract intellect that leave the heart cold
and dead, a mechanism that converts religion into
a mere round of outward ceremonies." (*History
of the Christian Religion and the Church*, vol. v.
p. 381.)

I therefore sought unto some of the most pious
and unworldly men of the German race to learn
how to find the supreme good. I met with Ruysbroch, whose Christian activity was witnessed in
the fourteenth century. He loved to wander in
the forests of Grünthal, musing upon divine things,
and elevating his soul to God in holy contemplation. There is something in such a place that
inspires the soul with a spirit of worship. In this
august temple not made with human hands, when

a deep, solemn murmur is heard in the forest,
when the storm is abroad and the tempest is
high, and

> "The loud wind through the forest wakes,
>   With sound like ocean's roaring, wild and deep,
>   And in yon gloomy pines strange music makes,"

to the holy soul it is Nature's *Te Deum laudamus*,
inviting us to join her loud acclaim. Burns, in
whose nature the religious element was prominent,
says of such a scene, " This is my best season for
devotion; my mind is filled with a kind of enthusiasm to Him who walketh on the wings of the
wind." Thus Ruysbroch, abstracted from all creaturely objects, and in communion with God, loved
to adore him in the deep forest. Shall we inquire of him how we can banish the world from
our hearts, and reach a conscious fellowship with
the Deity? He tells us in one of his works,
(*Speculum Æternæ Salutis*,) " If thou rightly un-
derstandest the nature of love, thou wilt govern
thyself, and be able easily to overcome the world,
and wilt die daily to sin, and lead a life of striv-
ing after virtue. Only I require that your soul
should free itself entirely from all outward and

creaturely objects, and cling to them in no way; that it should freely enter into its own deepest recesses, so as to rise upward from this centre to God, in a total estrangement of this inmost centre from the world. From this centre of its being the soul should sink and lose itself in God. Strive after this alone, that thou become free from form and image — become master of thyself; so thou wilt be able, as often as thou choosest, to turn thy heart and eye upward, where thy treasure and thy heart are, and thou wilt preserve one life with him. Nor wilt thou suffer the grace of God to be idle, but from true love wilt exercise thyself heavenward, in praising God; below, in all forms of virtue and good action. And in whatever outward action thou art employed, let thy heart be free and disengaged from all, so that, as oft as thou choosest, thou mayst be able, through all and above all, to contemplate Him whom thou lovest."

It is the privilege of the redeemed soul to have a sense of the divine presence, an inward consciousness of the indwelling Spirit. The pure in heart see God. The way the soul does this is perhaps beyond expression — it is ineffable. Men

not remarkable for the depth or spirituality of their
religious experience have admitted that the soul
may reach an inward sense of God. David Hart-
ley, notwithstanding his materialistic bent of mind,
recognized the power of the soul to do this, and
denominates it *theopathy*, and declares that it is a
right and beneficial mental condition. It is infinitely removed from all fanaticism. God is every
where in space; and must his existence be to us
a mere abstract conception of the intellect, a mere
opinion? He is the great central Life, pervading
all things. There is nothing in the universe whose
existence is so real. May we not have his *felt*
presence? There is nothing so near to us as God.
May we not *feel* him near? May we not attain
to an actual experience of the divine? May not
the purified soul, by virtue of its relationship to the
infinite Spirit, lose itself in his ineffable light, and
be as certain that he dwells within us as we are
that the sun shines without us? To this question
let Tauler reply out of the depth of his own experience. He says in his sermon on the Kingdom
of God, " I have a power in my soul which enables
me to perceive God; I am as certain as that I

live, that nothing is so near to me as God. He is nearer to me than I am to myself. It is a part of his very essence that he should be nigh and present to me. He is also nigh and present to a stone or a tree, yet they do not know it. If a tree could know God, and perceive his presence as the highest of the angels perceives it, the tree would be as blessed as the highest angel. And it is because man is capable of perceiving God, and knowing how nigh God is to him, that he is better off than a tree. And he is more blessed or less blessed in the same measure as he is aware of the presence of God. It is not because God is in him, and so close to him, and he hath God, that he is blessed, but because he perceives God's presence, and knows and loves him; and such a one will feel that God's kingdom is nigh at hand."

It has appeared to me, while studying the history of the church, that the piety of the eminent Christian teachers of the mediæval period was of a deeper type than is often witnessed in a subsequent age. Such persons as Bernard of Clairvaux, Anselm, Richard of St. Victor, Raymond Lull, and others, are truly lights shining in a dark place.

The attempt to follow Christ in evangelical poverty, which was one of the most influential ideas of the times, led them farther in self-abandonment than many at present are willing to go. They also lived in a stormy period; and to find rest, the soul retired inward upon itself from the noise of the outward world. Notwithstanding the tendency to externalize religion, many a soul found Christ within, and humbly lived and walked with God. In spite of the general corruption of the monastic orders, the monastery was sometimes a peaceful and fertile island in a tempestuous sea, where the soul communed with heaven. No one ever loved Christ with a more glowing love than Raymond Lull. He relates how he sought for Christ in the outward rites of the dominant state religions of his age, and how he wandered into other lands in search of Him who only manifests himself within. He says, " Often have I sought thee on the cross, and my bodily eyes have not been able to find thee, although they have found thine image there, and a representation of thy death. And when I could not find thee with my bodily eyes, I have sought thee with the eye of my soul; and thinking on thee, my soul found thee; and when it found thee, my heart began immediately to warm with the glow of love, my eyes to weep, and my mouth to praise thee." (*Neander's History of Christianity and the Church*, vol. iv. p. 307.) It is not by roaming through distant lands that the longing soul finds Christ. The true pilgrimage is to travel by purity of heart into the centre of our being. There he manifests himself as he does not to the world.

The highest aim of the Christian teachers of the middle age, who were eminently versed in the principles of the interior life, and according to them the highest stage of Christian experience, was the contemplation of God. Plato had taught that there were realities lying beyond the reach of the senses, and had instructed the world to rise from the sensible, the mutable, the earthy, to the contemplation of the immutable and eternal. The state of contemplation was with many an ideal state, after which they longed without realizing it. Others professed to reach this exalted Christian position. This state of contemplation appears to me identical with what some persons, eminent for piety, and who have attained the highest results of Christian experience, have denominated recollection. Mr. Fletcher, of Madely, says, " Recollection is a dwelling within ourselves; being abstracted from the creature, and turned towards God. It is both inward and outward. Outward recollection consists in *silence* from all idle and superfluous words, and a wise disentanglement from the world, keeping to our own business, observing and following the order of God for ourselves, and shutting the ear against all curious and unprofitable matters. Inward recollection consists in shutting the door of the senses; in a deep attention to the presence of God; and in a continual care of entertaining holy thoughts for fear of spiritual idleness. Let it be calm and peaceable; and let it be lasting." (*Benson's Life of Fletcher*, p. 87.) In another place, Mr. Fletcher says, "Let us shut our eyes to the gilded clouds without us; let us draw inward, and search after God, if haply we may find him." (*Life of Fletcher*, p. 335.) This seems to be essentially the same as what Bernard of Clairvaux (born *anno* 1091) describes as the third and last stage of Christian experience, " where the spirit collects its energies within itself, and, so far as it is divinely sustained, divests itself of things human to rise to the contemplation of God. At this last stage the man attains to that which is the aim of all aims — the *experience* of the divine. That which is highest cannot be taught by words, but only revealed through the Spirit. No language can explain it; but we may by prayer and purity of heart attain to it after we have prepared ourselves for it by a worthy life." (*History of Christianity and the Church*, vol. iv. p. 372.) If we analyze this state of contemplation, as it was apprehended by these distinguished Christian teachers, we shall find that it was a state of inward purity. Sin, which alone can separate the soul from God, was removed. Self was renounced and crucified. The world, with all creaturely objects, was abandoned as a source of rest to the soul. God was loved supremely, above all his gifts, and for his own sake, as the most perfect Being. It was a state of abstraction, a withdrawal of the soul into itself from the world of sense. The soul is introverted, *collected* in itself. The thoughts, affections, and desires, instead of being divergent in every direction, are drawn in from the circumference, "and consolidated around some centre, and that centre is God." (*Upham's Life of Faith*, p. 427.) This abstraction from the objects of sense, which the devout Kempis calls *peaceful vacancy*, makes the heart a solitude where God dwells alone. The mind is occupied intently with the idea of God, which fills the whole soul, to the exclusion of every thing else. Every thought, every desire, every affection is centred upon him. God, in an ineffable manner, is directly present to the spirit. The soul, by a kind of divine enchantment, is fixed upon him, and loses itself in the abyss of the divine Life. It is to be remarked also, that this state of contemplation is the point where faith begins to be lost in sight, or more correctly where faith becomes intuition, which is its most exalted form. Faith is the substance, or confident expectation, of things hoped for, the evidence, the convincing proof or demonstration, of things not seen. As Mr. Wesley defines it, "It is a divine evidence and conviction of God, and of the things of God." Its office in the mental economy is to give us a knowledge of those things that lie beyond the circle of sensation. In its highest form it becomes an intuition of those realities that exist behind the veil of sense. This is the only form of faith which belongs to the celestial state. But the contemplative spirit, on the wings of inward purity, even in this earthly stadium of our redemption, may soar upward, leaving the material and sensuous behind, and antedate the intuitions of the life eternal.

The enjoyment of God in the profoundest depth of our being is characteristic of the experience of eminent saints in all ages. Enoch walked with God. Jehovah commands his servant Abraham, "Walk before me, and be thou perfect." David says, "I have set the Lord always before me." In the Happy Islands it was an habitual and permanent state. Never did the Spaniard, on arriving in the western world, search more earnestly for gold, than we did for God; and here faith grasps the God we seek. In the sacred solitude of the heart he manifests himself as he does not to an unbelieving world, who know him not. Each of the inhabitants can say with rapture with the spouse, "My beloved is mine, and I am his;" and with David, "O God, thou art my God." The soul appropriates the

Divinity with all his infinite attributes. Blessed is that man who can say, "O God, thou art *my* God." There is in those words all that can be conceived of immortal blessedness. The loftiest seraph finds all his bliss in uttering them. They measure the full extent of angelic bliss. He who can truly repeat them has found the supreme good, for which philosophy sought in vain. It makes of every spot a hallowed place. Every hour of conscious existence is holy time. Every day is exalted to the dignity of a Sabbath, while the Sabbath is not lowered to mere secular time, but elevated to its true divine significance. It makes a prison a palace, and the wide world a Paradise.

> "Should Fate command me to the farthest verge
> Of the green earth, to distant, barbarous climes,
> Rivers unknown to song; where first the sun
> Gilds Indian mountains, or his setting beam
> Flames on the Atlantic isles; 'tis nought to me,
> Since God is ever present, ever *felt*,
> In the void waste as in the city full;
> And where he vital breathes there must be joy."

9 *

CHAPTER IV.

THE ISLAND ANAPAUSIS, OR THE LAND OF REST.

*The Place described. — The Saints' Rest. — Baxter. — The
golden Fountain. — Loss of the selfish Will. — Prayer resolved into its Essence. — Inordinate Desire. — Rule of
Kempis. — Silent Prayer. — True Riches. — Complete Satisfaction of all the Needs of our Nature. — Desire of Wealth,
of Honor, of Knowledge. — The Affections reposing on the
infinite Good. — A Symbol of the Soul's Rest in God. —
Extract from an old Author.*

> "Now rest my long-divided heart,
>   Fixed on this blissful centre, rest;
> Nor ever from thy Lord depart;
>   With him, of every good possessed."

AFTER FINDING the Supreme Good, a few
days were spent in the island called Anapausis. So quiet a place I had never found.
Beneath the lofty trees of the forest, venerable with
the age of centuries, the hand of God had spread
mossy couches designed for repose. The sea was

calm and tranquil. The noise of its waves was hushed to stillness. No fierce winds ever swept over the peaceful spot. The air was clear and balmy, neither chilly nor uncomfortably hot. The deep, clear blue of the firmament was like eternity made visible. The very sunbeams, whose mellow light flooded the scene, seemed to sleep on the hill-sides. A beautiful stream glided noiselessly along. On its flowery banks, beneath the spreading branches of a lofty tree, a shepherd had brought his flock to rest at noon. The whole scene that spread out before me was like a heavenly vision. The outward world, glowing with quiet beauty, in its deep silence invited the soul to repose.

It was here that the soul found what has been thought generally to belong only to the heavenly sphere — the saints' rest, the rest that remains for the people of God. This rest is attained when the struggle of the human with the divine will ceases, and both become one. St. Paul defines it to be a ceasing from our own works as God did from his. It is attained by faith, "for we that have believed do enter into rest." (Heb. iv. 3.) Mr.

Baxter seems to have entertained correct conceptions of what constitutes this rest. The saints' rest, according to him, is a soul in the enjoyment of God, and whoever has attained to the possession of the soul's true inheritance in this life has found it. He defines the saints' rest to be "tne most perfect state of a Christian, or it is the perfect endless enjoyment of God by the perfected saints, according to the measure of their capacity." (*Saints' Everlasting Rest*, p. 25.) Just before this, he exhorts the reader "to take God in Christ for his only rest, and to fix his heart upon him above all." And he prays that our carnal minds may be made so spiritual, and our earthly hearts so heavenly, that loving him, and delighting in him, may be the work of our lives. Those that enjoy this rest, he remarks, "have chosen God for their only end and happiness. He that takes any thing else for his happiness is out of the way the first step." It is not the rest of inaction, the rest of a stone which ceases from all motion when it has attained its centre; "but it contains a sweet and constant action of all the powers of the soul in the enjoyment of God." It is not labored action, for the soul moves spontaneously in God as in its native element; like the eagle with outspread and motionless wings, which, far up in the heavenly ether, calmly floats in an ocean of light. Such motion is rest. The swan, one of the most beautiful creations of the divine hand, moves without labored effort upon the surface of the lake. Such is the rest of the soul. It is not like the dead stillness of the Sea of Sodom, in whose lifeless waters nothing stirs, but like the deep majestic river, which by its own gravity moves onward by night and by noon, till it is lost in the ocean. The saints' rest is the action of the soul's powers in the enjoyment of God, and may be attained in this life, but will be more perfectly realized in the heavenly state. That soul which has learned to rise from things seen and temporal to the enjoyment of the internal presence of God, is no stranger to the bliss of the immortal shores. He lives in God, and moves in God as tranquilly as a vapory mountain floats across the summer's sky.

In the Happy Islands the inhabitants have found rest after a long and stormy voyage.

"A rest where all the soul's desire
Is fixed on things above;
Where fear, and sin, and grief expire,
Cast out by perfect love."

Here is found what we had sought in philosophy, and what the various sects of philosophers
falsely promised — *perfect mental tranquillity* — a
peace not based upon outward things, and not
affected by any thing external, the profound rest of
the soul arising from the enjoyment of the supreme
good.

In the centre of the island was a golden fountain. Its waters were clear as crystal, and were
like those that flow from beneath the throne of
God. It was situated in a beautiful glen hemmed
in on three sides by towering cliffs. It was a solitude fit for the abode of Beauty itself. The water
did not rush over the sides of the fountain, but it
was always full, and no sounding line had ever
measured its fathomless depths. I had never found
so holy and delightful a place. By this fountain
stood the Divine Man. He beckoned to me, and
said, " Come unto me, all ye that labor and are
heavy laden, and I will give you rest. If any man
thirst, let him come unto me and drink, for who-

soever drinketh of the water that I shall give him shall never thirst; but the water that I shall give him shall be in him a well of water springing up into everlasting life." I approached the crystal pool, and drank from the golden cup he extended towards me. All my inward cravings subsided into a divine repose. Every desire for something which I did not possess at the present moment ceased. In the possession of the infinite good, the soul had all, and could neither ask nor think of any thing more. Long had my spirit wished to reach a state where it could say, "It is enough," or to reproduce the experience of the apostle Paul, who could say, "I have learned in whatsoever state I am, therewith to be content."

The highest state in religion is a destruction of the selfish will, so that our will, without losing its individual existence and activity, perfectly harmonizes with the will of God, just as two well-tuned musical strings mingle their sounds into one. This loss of the selfish will is the death of all inordinate desire. If we would enjoy the profoundest repose, we must cease to desire any thing not included in the will of God. Our useless wishes and rebellious desires mar the soul's tranquillity, as the falling of a bank of earth defiles the pure waters of a flowing stream. We may reach a position of the Christian life where we shall desire nothing except what the present moment affords — a state of entire satisfaction and contentment. We are not condemned to a state of perpetual thirst, like Tantalus, nor to the dominion of an eternal craving. Our largest desires may be filled. But how shall this be attained? The inhabitants of the island, which I was visiting, told me that I must give myself wholly to God, must lay my will at the foot of his throne, and take him for my only portion, imploring him, in his love and unerring providence, to manage all my interests for both worlds, to give me all that peace, and joy, and sweetness of love diffused through my whole being, and all those inward and outward crosses which may be necessary to this result. Then I ought to recognize in the divine arrangements of the *present moment*, exactly what the soul needs, and find in that expression of the will of God the sum and satisfaction of all my desires. Nothing more disturbs the inward calmness

of the spirit than a restless craving for something
we do not possess. These clamorous desires are
like a flock of harpies, whose infectious touch spoils
the feast the divine bounty has spread for us in the
present moment. We have in an omnipresent Deity,
and in that divine order of things his providence
has arranged for this moment, all we can need.
Why should the discontented soul wander abroad
for more? We have in the possession of the Infinite One the chief ingredient in the cup of angelic
bliss. We have in him all we can find in wealth,
or honor, or health; all that is valuable in society
and friends, or home and country.

The farther a soul advances in holiness, and the
more complete is its recovery from the ruins of the
fall, the more prayer will be resolved into its essence,
which is the all-comprehensive desire, finding its
appropriate utterance in the petition, " Thy will be
done in earth as it is in heaven." The nearer one
is advanced towards the borders of the celestial
realms, the less prayer will busy itself with particular requests; the less it will ask for particular
gifts. I was informed by the people who inhab-
ited the Island of Anapausis, that when they kneel

down to pray in those holy retreats, with which the country abounds, they sometimes find they can only ask for God. After drinking of the waters of the fountain of life, and getting a taste of the divine and heavenly, they can say with David, "Whom have I in heaven but thee? and there is none upon the earth I desire beside thee." Prayer spontaneously goes in search for God. Every desire naturally fixes itself upon him. The soul wants nothing separate from God. If any particular object, of which it may conceive, is contrary to God, the heart does not desire it; if it be less than God, it will not satisfy the needs of our nature. This is what Catharine Adorna calls the annihilation of desire. It is more properly every desire finding rest in the infinite Good, and becoming sweetly fixed upon the universal Centre. The restless activity of the desires has ceased, rather than the desires themselves. He who would attain to the deepest tranquillity must not only lay down his will at Jesus' feet, but must also deposit there every desire of his spirit. This is what Kempis means in his favorite precept, which may truly be called a golden rule — "Part with all, and thou shalt find all. Relinquish desire, and thou shalt find rest."

In the holy stillness of this land of rest, over which broods a perpetual Sabbath, the soul finds itself much inclined to what the devout Scougal calls *mental* prayer — a prayer which can only be offered in adoring silence, as it is too deep for utterance, and to which St. Paul perhaps has a special reference when he speaks of the " Spirit helping our infirmities, and making intercession for us, with groanings which cannot be uttered," or, as the original will bear, *cannot be worded.* This is the sublimest form of prayer. The soul, swelling with ineffable desires, in the profoundest adoration, holds itself with speechless awe in the divine presence, and reposes on the bosom of Divinity, filled with all the silent heaven of love. This form of prayer, though it is not to be practised at all times to the exclusion of every other, has this advantage over vocal prayer, that the mind is more concentrated or recollected. The spirit retires behind the veil of the senses, abstracts itself wholly from the outward world, turns inward upon itself, and adores God in the inner chamber of the heart.

This is worshipping him in spirit and in truth. In silent prayer the Deity is brought inconceivably near. Faith goes and raps on the door of God's interior sanctuary, where he dwells alone, concealed from the gaze of the sensuous host without. He opens the door; the soul enters, and is shut in with God. Perhaps but few can wholly leave the outward world, become free from its images, and retire into the spirit's profoundest recess, shutting the world out, and the Deity in. That hour is full of blessedness when the soul. has such audience with its Maker; when it thus leaves a noisy world, and is present with the Lord. It is next to going to heaven. It is heaven begun. How sweet to obey the command, " Be still, and know that I am God"! In such an hour, when every desire is hushed to silence by an unutterable satisfaction, the soul experiences a fulfilment of the words of Jesus in John xvi. 23 —" In that day ye shall ask me nothing;" or, as Bloomfield renders it, "In that day ye shall have nothing to ask me." That is, such is the fulness of a soul lost in God, that it has nothing more to ask, nothing to desire. Want has fled from the spirit.

The Infinite and finite have flowed together, and the soul shares the unutterable tranquillity of the divine mind. The soul receives what Christ in his dying legacy left to his church. " Peace I leave with you; *my* peace I give unto you. Not as the world giveth, give I unto you." (John xiv. 27.) It was the same peace which Jesus himself enjoyed, and which he brought back from its flight to heaven, to dwell once more on earth. It is heaven pouring itself into the emptiness of the human spirit. It is what Paul speaks of as entering into the rest of God, partaking the calm repose of the divine Mind. This divine rest is not always an emotional state. It is an inexpressible stillness of spirit, like that which reigns outside the bounds of creation, in the solitude of empty space, where there is nothing but the all-pervading Deity. It is a purely spiritual state, almost a disembodied state. It is like a fathomless ocean in a calm. This profound inward repose shows itself in the calm placidity of the countenance. In the Happy Islands, the outward form of the people is made effusive of the peace within. The face becomes the very effigy of divine peace.

10 *

The outward man is moulded into the image of the inner man, and the clay tabernacle gleams with celestial peace, like a distant palace glittering with the rays of a setting sun, or like a mountain summit, which rises like a majestic column of light amid the growing darkness.

Society in the Happy Islands resembled the fellowship of heaven. In the world they had left behind there was a universal struggle, night and day, for wealth. This restless craving for riches, this insatiable lust for gain, was a consuming fire to all peace of mind, and engendered a thousand crimes. But here all had attained the true riches in the possession of God. "No determinate sum of gold, nor quantity of estate, can make a man rich, since no man is truly rich that has not so much as perfectly satiates his desire of having more. For the desire of more is want, and want is poverty." (*Meditations of Hon. Charles How.*) Here none were poor. I here learned a lesson which would have been worth a voyage round the globe to acquire — *that he is not rich who has much, but he who desires little.* He who desires nothing is infinitely rich. To grow rich is not to add to our possessions, but to subtract from our desires. In the Happy Islands, the fruitful root of crime was destroyed. Here were no wars, or quarrels, or litigations; no thefts or robberies, or murders, and no oppression of the poor. Earthly things seemed empty and vain.

> "As by the light of opening day
>   The stars are all concealed,
> So earthly pleasures fade away,
>   When Jesus is revealed.
>
> Creatures no more divide my choice;
>   I bid them all depart;
> His name, his love, his gracious voice
>   Have fixed my roving heart."

The rest which was here enjoyed consisted in the complete satisfaction of all the wants of our being. The desire of possession, which is a fruitful source of disquiet in the world, and which earthly things can never satisfy, because the desire is nourished and strengthened by the increase of our possessions, here found its appropriate centre in the supreme good. He who attempts to satisfy this propensity with created things, which are empty of God, is like the shipwrecked sailor, who attempts to quench the raging thirst, which consumes him, with the waters of the ocean on which he floats. A few drops from the heavens would avail more than the whole Pacific to allay his burning thirst. The desire of honor, the thirst for glory, can be satisfied only with the conscious approbation of God. The lowest station in life gratifies our love of honor as well as the highest. The man who rises from the common walks of life to the summit of worldly honor and power, is like the man who ascends the top of the lofty mountain which looks so tranquil as it leans against the heavens. He rises from the valley where flowers grow and birds sing, leaves the last trace of vegetation below, and enters the region of perpetual congelation, where tempests howl forever around the throne of eternal winter. The intellect can never rest until it has attained the true knowledge of God. All the treasures of ancient philosophy and modern lore cannot fill the desire to know which is inherent in our nature. "Let not the wise man glory in his wisdom; but let him that glorieth glory in this, that he understandeth and knoweth me, that I am the Lord." (Jer. ix. 23, 24. The affections can repose with satisfaction only upon God. A susceptibility of exercising love is one of the most valuable powers of our nature. But to prevent this emotion from being a source of disquietude, and not of rest, the object loved must be of sufficient worth and excellence to answer the vastness of the capacity. Love soon stretches itself beyond every created object. It is an emotion that was made for God, and nothing less than infinite moral beauty can give it rest — can afford it room to expand and exert all its vigor and activity. But when the most perfect Being is the object on which it fixes, it may expend all its energy. It can never outgrow such an object. To confine our love to the creatures is to experience an unsatisfied craving continually, and will be a source of more torment than peace. Wouldst thou find repose of soul? Love the infinite Good. Love all other things, even thyself, for his sake, and thou shalt find rest. Created things are to be loved as radiations of the divine Life.

Again, love is restless without the presence of the object loved. When the beloved object is far removed, the soul feels the pang and chasm of separation. The soul cries out, " Make haste, my beloved, and be like a roe, or a young hart, on the spicy mountains." How happy, then, are those who supremely love Him who can never be absent from them. He would cease to be God if he ceased to be every where present. Love must *possess* God, or never be at rest. Pure love is disinterested, and asks no reward except the object loved. And this it always has. It is not possible to our nature to love an object, and not desire to possess it. The soul that loves God requires God in return. It never can rest until it can say with the spouse, from an inward sense and experience, " My Beloved is mine." How happy the soul which can say, in e rapture of perfect love, " This God is our God forever and ever." O the immensity of this possession !

> " Earth flies with all the charms it has in store;
> Its snares and gay temptations are no more;
> Creatures no more of entity can boast ;
> The streams, the hills, the towering groves are lost.
> The sun, the stars, and the fair fields of light
> Withdraw, and now are banished from my sight,
> And God is all in all."

To create a soul capable of loving God, and

yet to keep that soul in the distance, is to make a being that is restless from the necessity of his nature and situation. In the Happy Islands he infinitely shortens the distance between himself and our ransomed souls. It is thought by some philosophers, that in the material world no two bodies ever actually touch, however near they may approach to each other. But the holy soul comes into contact with the infinite Spirit. He is above all, for the universe cannot contain him; he is through all, for his essence pervades all things; and he is in all who love him. It is this conscious indwelling of the Divinity that can alone give rest to the soul. Hence, says Dr. Cudworth, "*Deus ipse, sum omni sua bonitate, quatenus extra me est, non facit beatum, sed quatenus in me est*" — *God himself, with all his goodness, so far as he is without me, cannot make me blessed, but only so far as he is in me.* In the Happy Islands there seems to be nothing but God. The soul is made one with him in everlasting love. The spirit rises to its source on a flame of love as inextinguishable as the fires of heaven, and oftentimes loses itself in the All. Says Mrs.

Elizabeth Rowe, " How calm, how peaceful, in those seasons are all the regions of my soul! I have enough, I ask no more. Can they languish for the stream who drink at the overflowing fountain? I have all the world and more! I have heaven itself in thee; in thee I am completely and securely blessed, and can defy the malice of earth and hell to shake the foundation of my happiness, while thou dost whisper thy love to my soul. O blessed stability of heart! O sublime satisfaction!" (*Devout Exercises of the Heart*, p. 41.)

This state of divine repose which the soul finds in communion with the Deity, seems to be that recommended by Michael de Molinos, a Spanish priest, who, in a book entitled the Spiritual Guide, which he published in the year 1681, taught that the highest state in religion consists in the perfect tranquillity of a mind removed from all external and finite things, and centred in God, and in a pure and perfect love of him for his own sake, as intrinsically lovely, independent of all his dealings with us. This holy quietism, this heavenly sabbatism, was enjoyed in the Island of Anapausis.

Here the spirit attained a rest so profound, so far below the world, in the abyss of Deity, that nothing could disturb the deep repose of the soul. It is difficult to describe it in words, for it is the peace of God that passeth all understanding. It may be presented to the mind under the image of a boundless ocean, with all its clouds and storms cleared away, and its restless heavings subsided into a motionless placidity. Over this is seen nothing but the blue concave, like the curtain of eternity, filled with a mild light, which rests upon the sea and illumines its surface. No sun, nor moon, nor stars, are seen. No land appears in view. Far out of sight of the world, and all its false show, and out of hearing of its noise, a cross is seen on the surface of the calm, waveless deep. On it there rests a sleeping infant with nought to disturb its innocent repose. Such rest have holy souls in Christ.

He who would find rest to his spirit must abandon all created things as objects of supreme affection, and must live under the very walls of heaven, so that its immortal bliss shall flow over and fill his soul. All this he will enjoy in a state of inward union with God. In a little work on the Perfect Life, by an unknown author, published about the year 1350, the writer attempts to show that it is possible for the soul, even while it is yet in the body, to reach so high as to cast a glance into eternity, and receive a foretaste of eternal life and eternal blessedness. But in order for the soul to rise to such a state, " she must be quite pure, wholly stripped and bare of all images, and be entirely separate from all creatures, and especially from herself. And as soon as a man turneth himself in spirit, and with his whole heart and mind entereth into the mind of God, which is above all time, all that ever he hath lost is restored in a moment; that is, the original divine fellowship which man enjoyed in paradise, before it was lost through sin, is brought back to his soul. And if a man were to do thus a thousand times in a day, each time a fresh and real union would take place; and in this sweet and divine work standeth the truest and fullest union that may be in this present time. For he who hath attained thereto asketh nothing further; for he hath found the kingdom of heaven and eternal life on earth." (*Theologia Germanica*, pp. 22, 23.)

> "There's quiet in the deep:
> Above, let tides and tempests rave,
> And earthborn whirlwinds wake the wave;
> Above, let care and fear contend
> With sin and sorrow to the end:
> Here, far beneath the tainted foam
> That frets above our peaceful home,
> We dream in joy, and wake in love,
> Nor know the rage that yells above.
>
> There's quiet in the deep."

CHAPTER V.

A DARK DAY AT THE HAPPY ISLANDS.

Day of Trial. — Darkness of naked Faith. — Virtue struggling with opposing Powers. — The Reason of these spiritual combats. — The Christian Life a Reappearance of the Life of Jesus in the Soul. — The Childhood of Jesus. — Wilderness State. — Poverty of Christ experienced. — His Servant Form. — His Peace and Joy. — Sympathy with the final Hour of Jesus. — Harmony between the outward World and the World within. — Results of the Trial. — The Darkness ends. — The Day breaks.

THERE WAS one feature of the climate of the Happy Islands that I had not expected to find. Every day since my arrival, the sun had risen with unsurpassed splendor, and had never been obscured by a cloud. The nights were as delightful as the day. The moon and stars shone with increased splendor, so that the whole land was flooded with their mild radiance. It seemed a fulfilment of the prophecy, "Thy sun shall no more go down, nor thy moon withdraw itself; for the Lord shall be thine everlasting light, and the days of thy mourning shall be ended." (Isa. lxi. 21.) There seemed to be a realization of the state of the church described in Rev. xxii. 5 — "And there shall be no night there, and they need no candle, neither light of the sun, for the Lord God giveth them light, and they shall reign forever and ever." The soul had floated in an ocean of uncreated light; it had been given it,

> "With the deep-transported mind, to soar
> Above the wheeling poles, and at heaven's door
> Look in."

It was well there should be a day of trial. And I learned from the inhabitants that occasionally the islands were enveloped in a profound darkness, when neither sun, nor moon, nor stars could be seen; a midnight strange, such as nature shuddered to behold. It was observed one morning, after an unusually brilliant sunrise, that the sun grew pale. This continued to increase, until, through the gloomy haze, only the outline of its disk could be faintly discerned. The heavens were

11 *

still; all nature was silent. There were no clouds
that rushed angrily across the sky; no storm
raved around. A peculiar solemnity brooded over
all things. At length the sun wholly disappeared,
and the eye could not trace its position in the
heavens. It became so dark that objects could be
discerned only with difficulty. The sun was black
as sackcloth of hair. It brought to mind a passage in the prophet Ezekiel: "When I shall put
thee out, I will cover the heaven, and make the
stars thereof dark; I will cover the sun with a
cloud, and the moon shall not give her light. All
the bright lights of heaven will I make dark over
thee, and set darkness upon thy land, saith the
Lord God." (Ezek. xxxii. 7, 8.) I could say,
with Job, "I went mourning without the sun; I
stood up and cried in the congregation." (Job
xxx. 28.) There was such a day of darkness in
Palestine, and throughout the world, eighteen centuries ago — a day of darkness and the shadow of
death, a dread eclipse, without opposing spheres.
The people of the islands called such seasons the
Darkness of naked Faith.

In this midnight gloom the soul was assailed

by the spirits of darkness, which I had supposed never had an existence in this happy region. I had thought that virtue here had to encounter no hostile forces. While I wondered at finding myself surrounded by principalities and powers, and wicked spirits in heavenly places, a divine voice seemed to roll through the past centuries, and reach my ear—"Think it not strange concerning the fiery trial which is to try you, as though some strange thing had happened unto you; but rejoice, inasmuch as ye are made partakers of Christ's sufferings, that when his glory shall be revealed, ye may be glad with exceeding joy." (1 Pet. iv. 12, 13.) The reason why the powers of darkness were permitted to invade these peaceful and holy scenes, was afterwards fully understood. The aim of the divine administration is the creation of the greatest amount of holiness, and the consequent happiness, in the universe. This end is kept steadily in view in the government of free agents, and unerring wisdom adopts all the means necessary to secure this result. The inhabitants of the islands desired to avail themselves of all the redemptive agencies, in order

to reach the highest degree of holiness. Now the
most exalted form of virtue, in this stage of our
existence, is virtue struggling with opposing powers, and taking up arms against a host of hostile
influences. Hence Adam was tempted in Paradise.
Hence, in order to exhibit the holiness of the
character of Jesus in its most intense aspect, he
was assailed by all the forces of hell. But behold, in this struggle of free will against the gates
of hell, the most exalted form of holiness. In this
struggle the soul grows strong, just as the inhabitants of the Sandwich Islands believed that the
strength of an enemy slain in battle passed into
the victor. The object of a probationary discipline is the establishment in the free agent of
fixed habits of holiness. Every temptation, success-
fully encountered, serves to settle the soul in its
Christian position. Hence the perfect man of Uz
had to encounter the principle of evil. Abraham,
also, the friend of God, was severely tried. His
virtue was subjected to a fiery test, in order that
it might not be a mere surface coloring, but might
strike through into the very texture of the soul.
He who desires to be holy in the highest possible

degree, and sees in temptation a means to such an end, will learn to obey the precept, "Count it all joy when ye fall into divers temptations;" like soldiers striking their shields against their spears, and rushing to battle with shouts and songs. It seemed to me, during this day of darkness, that the experience so vividly described by David was reproduced: "Be not far from me, for trouble is near; for there is none to help. Many bulls have compassed me; strong bulls of Bashan have beset me round. They gaped upon me with their mouths, as a ravening and roaring lion. I am poured out like water, and all my bones are out of joint; my heart is like wax; it is melted in the midst of my bowels. My strength is dried up like a potsherd; and my tongue cleaveth to my jaws; and thou hast brought me into the dust of death." (Ps. xxii. 11–15.)

The Christian life, in its profoundest import, not as something outward, not as a series of external actions, is a following of Christ. It is a reappearance, in the interior experience of the disciple, of the different states of the Master. It is a putting on of Christ — an expression borrowed from the ancient stage. It is Christ formed within. We must pass through the childhood of Jesus. For except a man be converted, and become as a little child, he cannot enter into the kingdom of God. For that kingdom is not entered by motion through space, as you would pass into the domains of an earthly monarch, but by the possession of holy dispositions and tempers. We must possess the believing, confiding, humble, and docile temper of the child Jesus, who increased in wisdom and favor, both with God and men. The innocent attributes of childhood must be restored to our fallen souls. " He that shall humble himself, as this little child, shall be great in the kingdom of heaven."

There was the temptation of Christ in the wilderness. As the Messiah, in the early part of his ministry, was led into the desert, so every disciple, in the early stage of his experience of the higher, hidden life of Christianity, must pass into a wilderness state. The restored spirit must be disciplined for a higher and holier flight into the enjoyment of the Deity. Our love must be purified from all taint of earth and self, so that it shall ascend a pure, seraphic flame, without smoke or earthy vapor, and the heart shall become a golden lamp, burning perpetually before the throne of God. Pure love is not so much an emotion as a fixed state of a will in harmony with God. An excited state of the pleasurable emotions is not the highest position in religion. There is a more commanding standing ground — one farther inward from the circumference towards the great central Life. In entering upon the higher life, the soul must learn to love holiness for its own intrinsic excellence, and not merely as a means of exciting in us blissful ecstasies. The first feature of the wilderness state is a cessation of all the pleasurable emotions of the soul. The heart sometimes experiences a state it is not easy to describe. There is no emotion of any kind, no active desire, no joy, no conscious peace, no misery, no guilt. There is a suspension of the soul's sensibility. A desert is not more destitute of flowers than is the spirit of emotions. It is a state of inward emptiness. It is not necessarily an unhappy condition. The soul is like the clear blue vault of heaven on a winter day, when no cloud is seen, and no winds are abroad. This absence of emotion may be a "peaceful vacancy," though we are often alarmed; just as a traveller on a lonely mountain summit sometimes is terrified at the very silence which there reigns. It seems more dreadful to him than the loudest thunder. This inward stillness is often attended with a restless and painful longing, and with an apprehension that God has abandoned us; the soul, in its blindness, having taken the gifts of God for himself. If we set ourselves to enjoy the highest results of the Christian experience, and to be wholly the Lord's, the question must soon be settled, whether we love God as a means of our happiness, or for his own sake. If we can be satisfied with nothing but the intoxication of emotion, we give him an altogether secondary place in our affections; we make him only a means of our enjoyment, instead of sacrificing ourselves to him. Such a soul has not fully lost itself in God. We should aim to realize what was called by Archbishop Fenelon a state of pure love — a disinterested love, a love of *order, of absolute beauty, and perfection,* superior to every agreeable sensation, and which can act in the

absence of all the sensible pleasures and consolations of grace. The soul, at such a time, may have
no feeling, no happy emotion, on which its faith
may lean. Yet it still holds to God, and loves
him for his own sake above all his gifts. It is
conscious, in its profoundest depths, of a refined
satisfaction with God and complacency in him.
The love that exists in such a state of naked faith
is the purest form of Christian love. It has less
of self in it. The finite recedes, and the Infinite
fills the affections. It is as pure as the breeze
that fans an angel's brow. It may not be an
emotion. It is deeper than an emotion. We are
told that there are depths of the ocean where the
plummet sinks below all the currents and disturb-
ances of the surface, and where eternal stillness
reigns. So of the soul in this state of naked faith
and pure love. It is an angelic flame, still and
silent as the unfathomed depth of the sea. A state
of naked faith, or what some writers on inward
experience denominate the wilderness state, is a
most beneficial mental condition, if the spirit does
not falter, and if the will holds the soul, emptied
of all desires and emotions, in the presence of God.

We should not be seized with a panic, nor struggle to work ourselves into an emotional frame. If the enemy insultingly asks, Where is now thy God? stand like Christ before the bar of Pilate in triumphant silence; or, if you speak, let praise flow from your lips like melody from the string. Alas, how many stumble and fall when the divine Shepherd leads them into the desert, to wean them from themselves and the world, and purge from the soul all its sensuous and earthy images! This is the crisis in the experience of the hidden life. It is a spiritual Rubicon. If we cross it, victory and empire await us in the future.

After Christ had been in the wilderness without bread for forty days, " his soul was an hungered." So we must remain in the desert until our craving for God shall become so intense, that, overlooking all his gifts, we shall ask only for himself.

The poverty of Christ, his looseness from the world and the things of earth, must be reproduced by the disciple. The Son of Man had not where to lay his head. The follower of Jesus must pass through a similar state. Though in the midst of wealth and honors, he must experience their emptiness and vanity, and divest his heart of the love of them. He must inwardly forsake all, and emptied of the creatures, which can never satisfy the yearnings of his higher nature, the abyss of the soul must echo with the cry for the supreme Good. "Blessed are the poor in spirit, for theirs is the kingdom of heaven." Genuine Christ-like poverty is more an inward than an outward condition. Some have erred here. In the age of Constantine, when, with all the means at the disposal of a despotic prince, he heaped riches and honors upon the church, a strange enthusiasm seized a portion of the Christian mind of the times to reproduce the unworldly spirit and poverty of Christ. This vast movement of the Christian spirit had its uses in the scheme of the Messiah's providence, in counteracting the worldly tendency of the church; yet there was an error at bottom. It is not so much the outward form of the Redeemer's poverty, as his poverty of spirit, that is to be experienced by his followers. Monachism erred in fleeing to the solitudes of the desert in order to reproduce the poverty of Christ. It may be experienced on a throne.

The Divinity, as he appeared in Christ, assumed the form of a servant, and performed the most menial offices, even washing the feet of the disciples. He hints to his followers that they should imitate his servant form, especially in its inward spirit, when he says, on laying aside the towel with which he was girded, " What I do ye know not now, but ye shall know hereafter." This state must be experienced. This state of condescending love must be a permanent one, and coeval with the whole Christian life. It appears in the very first breathings of the new Christian spirit — a spirit of love, a desire to call down upon the head of every living being the blessing of God, and to wring out to every soul of man a full cup of blessedness.

> " O that the world might taste and see
> The riches of his grace!
> The arms of love that compass me
> Would all mankind embrace."

For the perfection of the human spirit, and its perfect discipline for the enjoyment of the life eternal, it must be a partaker of all the different states of Christ. In the light of this truth, how beautifully appears his promise to his disciples just before his departure from the world!—" Peace I leave with you; *my* peace I give unto you. Not as the world giveth, give I unto you." That is, this is not a mere empty form of valediction, or farewell, like the customary adieu, or good by, but a real inward peace and solid repose, a reproduction in your soul of the calm tranquillity and divine serenity of my own heart. The joy of Christ is also to be experienced by the disciple. " These things I speak in the world, that they might have my joy fulfilled in themselves." (John xvii. 13.) In another place he says, " These things have I spoken unto you, that my joy might remain in you, and that your joy might be full." (John xv. 11.)

We are now prepared to see that the disciple who gives himself up to follow the Master whithersoever he goeth, must sooner or later be crucified with Christ, or share the agony of the final hour of Jesus. He must not only ride with him in triumph into Jerusalem, and share the glory of the theocratic king, but must sympathize with his atoning death struggle. This is necessary in order to rise into the highest degree of Christian life. He must bear about in his body the dying of the Lord Jesus, in order that the life also of Jesus may be made manifest in our mortal flesh. It was not the thorns, not the nails, nor the unfeeling scoffs of a heartless mob, that made up the sum of his sufferings in the final hour. These were but a drop in his sad cup. It was the withdrawal of the conscious presence of his Father. "This was the finishing stroke of the hand of God that smote that Man of Sorrows. This was what con-summated the sacrifice." It was this that extorted the exclamation, "My God, my God, why hast thou forsaken me? Why art thou so far from helping me, and from the words of my roaring?" (Ps. xxii. 1.) So the believer must pass through a state of internal anguish, obscurity, and *apparent* abandonment of God. We must taste something of the deep soul-agony of Gethsemane and Calvary. We shall experience a withdrawal of all sensible divine comfort, and the soul must be thrown upon its own resources. This is the severest trial of

the whole Christian life. To rejoice that we are
made partakers of Christ's sufferings is the hardest
lesson a Christian has to learn in the school of
Christ; yet it may be learned at the feet of Jesus.
Says Kempis, "It requires no considerable effort
to despise human consolation, when we are possessed of divine. But it is transcendent greatness
to bear the want of both, and without self-condo-
lence, or the least retrospection on our own imaginary worth, patiently to suffer desolation of heart
for the glory of God." (*Imitation of Christ*, p. 94.)
This is a kind of spiritual martyrdom, an inward
crucifixion. It is preëminently referred to in Rom.
viii. 17, where we are said to be heirs of God,
and joint heirs with Christ, if so be that we suffer
with him, that we may be also glorified together.
Happy the man whose desolate spirit, while passing through those deaths and hells that sometimes
accompany the birth of the soul into a higher
stage of life, can say, "Though he slay me, yet
will I trust in him." Like as Christ entered into
rest through the suffering of death, so the soul
that thus trusts God in this gloomy hour will rejoice to find that by subduing his earthly and

selfish nature, it yields to him a rich harvest of divine peace.

During this day of darkness at the Happy Islands, there was a complete harmony between the outward world and the world within. This I found was always the case during my stay in the country. When God withdraws his conscious presence, nature is clothed in gloom. Nothing can cheer the soul, not even the smiles of angels. I could say with David, "Thou didst hide thy face, and I was troubled." (Ps. xxx. 7.) Yet my soul could say with confidence, as it turned its imploring gaze upward to Him

"Whose throne is darkness in the abyss of light,
A flood of glory which forbids the sight,"—

"Thou wilt light my candle; the Lord my God will enlighten my darkness." (Ps. xviii. 28.) Though the earth was without form and void, and darkness was upon the face of the deep, yet I rejoiced to know that the Spirit of God was moving upon the face of the waters. I patiently waited the time when the creative word should go forth, Let there be light, and then light would flash amid the chaos. The spirit felt, as never before, that God was its supreme good. In this temporary removal of his *manifested* presence, it saw how necessary he was to its rest. His gifts would not suffice. The last tie that bound the heart to earthly and finite good was broken. I was dead, and my life was hid with Christ in God. It was ever deemed the best day of my religious history. It demonstrated the strength of my love. At a time when it has appeared to others that they did not love God at all, because of the absence of the emotion of love, and of the sensible presence of God, it seemed to me that I never loved him so much. Love never shows itself so strong as when called upon to separate from its adored object. In this *apparent* departure of God from the soul, its very misery arises from the strength of its love. If it does not love God, why this all-absorbing desire for his return? Why this intense longing to be with him, so that we can say, "My soul longeth, yea, even fainteth for the courts of the Lord. When shall I come and appear before God?" Why does the fond spirit say to Him it adores, when fearing his absence, —

"Stay, my beloved, with me here;
Stay till the morning star appear;
Stay till the dusky shadows fly
Before the day's illustrious eye."

The heart of the wicked says, in its want of affinity for God, and its instinctive repugnance to the divine, " Depart from me, for I desire not the knowledge of thy ways." The repulsion between a depraved nature and the Holy One led the demoniac of Gadara to say, " What have I to do with thee, Jesus, thou Son of God." But the spouse, in the absence of him whom her soul loved could say, " I will arise now, and go about the city, and in the broad ways; I will seek him whom my soul loveth." In withdrawing from the soul his conscious presence, and bringing it into the shadow of death, God aims both to test the strength of its love, and to increase it. Blessed is that heart which has learned this truth, and can distinguish between pleasurable emotions and God, between a peace which is the gift of God and the God of peace. That day brought the soul into a more intimate union with its divine Centre. From that era the veil that separated my spirit from the Deity became exceedingly transparent, and the

Invisible appeared in sight. During this horror of great darkness that settled like a curtain of sackcloth over the land, there were occasionally flashes of light. Sometimes a promise broke through the gloom, like a star looking from behind a midnight cloud. This passage flashed out upon the darkened heavens — "There is but a moment in his anger; in his favor is life; weeping may endure for a night, but joy cometh in the morning." (Ps. xxx. 5.) These gleams of light became increasingly frequent, until a whole constellation of divine promises was hung out in the heavens by the hand of God, as darkness shows us worlds of light we never saw by day. At length the dismal curtain over the heavens exhibited numerous rents. The celestial light leaked through. The gloomy funereal pall was lifted at last from the western horizon, and the divine Artist painted on the black canvas the bow of many colors, the sign of the covenant, and the symbol of peace. So glorious a sunset my eyes never beheld.

> "Confusion hears his voice, and wild uproar
> Stands ruled, and at his bidding, darkness flies,
> Light shines, and order from disorder springs."

The night following was one of unusual brilliancy. The Aurora marched across the Heavens. The moon serenely floated in the pure ether. The heavens proclaimed the glory of God, and the earth seemed full of his riches. The transition from such a night to the following day was hardly perceptible. Above the melody of the spheres there came a voice to the soul, — God is all.

> "There's not a tint that paints the rose,
>   Or decks the lily fair,
>   Or streaks the humblest flower that grows,
>   But Heaven has placed it there.
>
>   There's not of grass a single blade,
>   Or leaf of lowliest mien,
>   Where heavenly skill is not displayed,
>   And heavenly wisdom seen.
>
>   There's not a cloud whose dews distil
>   Upon the parchéd clod,
>   And clothe with verdure vale and hill,
>   That is not sent by God.
>
>   There's not a star whose twinkling light
>   Illumes the distant earth,
>   And cheers the solemn gloom of night,
>   But Heaven gave it birth.
>
>   There's not a place in earth's vast round,
>   In ocean's depths, or air,

Where skill and wisdom are not found,
  For God is every where.

Around, beneath, below, above,
  Wherever space extends,
There heaven displays its boundless love,
  And power with goodness blends."

13

CHAPTER VI.

THE ISLAND OF EUPHROSYNE.

The Scenery. — The Appearance of the outward World depends upon the State of the Soul. — Effect of Melancholy. — Peace, Joy, Purity. — The Art of being always happy. — Ceaseless Praise. — Rejoicing in the Lord. — The Desert becomes a fruitful Field. — The Valley of Baca filled with Pools. — The Triumph of Habakkuk. — A Plant which symbolizes such a State. — St. Paul. — The Mount of Purity. — Perennial Springs. — Enrapturing View from the Summit. — What a Mountain symbolizes. — Effect of the View upon the Soul. — Quotation from Baxter.

EARLY IN the morning after the dark day, I crossed over to the Island Euphrosyne. It is one of the most delightful of the whole group —a land of joy, favored with God's peculiar smile. The morning was clear and bright. Birds of sweetest song filled the skies with their melody. A thousand varieties of flowers, scattered over the meadows and pastures, flung their odors to the passing breezes, and perfumed the whole land. Beds of violets, hedges of fresh-blown roses, clusters of orange trees in blossom, were seen beside the roads, and on the banks of brooks that flowed joyfully along. These beautiful rivulets, rolling musically over their pebbly beds, flowed by cottages, and through neat and highly cultivated gardens, and sometimes under triumphal arches of flowering vines. Here I saw the lambs in their innocent gambols around the kind shepherd. The shouts of happy childhood greeted the ear; the winds sported with the leaf, and the sunbeams glittered in the dewdrops. Above all was heard, in every direction, songs of praise which ascended from a thousand hearts, for it was the hour of morning prayer. All the joyful voices of nature, and the music of human voices which were mingled together, did not sound like boisterous mirth. The whole was·chastened and hallowed by the presence of God, which brooded over the scene. These appearances of the outward world seemed to be the pulsations of God's infinite heart of joy. It was the bliss of the divine Mind, overflowing in cheerful creations of his hand. Every thing has a charm to the holy soul, if it sees a present Deity in it.

> "It is his presence that diffuses charms
> Unspeakable, o'er mountain, wood, and stream.
> To think that He, who hears the heavenly choirs,
> Hearkens complacent to the woodland song;
> To think that He, who rolls yon solar sphere,
> Uplifts the warbling songster to the sky;
> To mark his presence in the mighty bow
> That spans the clouds as in the tints minute
> Of tiniest flower; to hear his awful voice
> In thunder speak, and whisper in the gale;
> To know and feel his care for all that lives;
> 'Tis this that makes the barren waste appear
> A fruitful field, each grove a paradise!"

In this island were forests of trees whose leaf never withered. The hills were clothed in unfading green. The tall, graceful palm was found in abundance, which gave to the scenery an air of perpetual triumph. This majestic tree has some peculiarities which fit it for its symbolical use as the emblem of victory and joy. Plutarch tells us that it was its natural property to rise up against pressure, so that it flourished in proportion to the weights attached to it to depress it. It retains also its youthful vigor to an extreme age, so that the ancients accounted it immortal, or at least, if

it did die, it recovered again, and obtained a
second life by renewal. It, moreover, belongs
to the class of plants that do not grow from external accretions, but from internal additions. It
grows from the centre outwards. With what propriety does the Psalmist say, "The righteous shall
flourish as the palm tree." (Ps. xciii. 12.) There
were other trees on the island, but this was the
prevailing one, and gave character to the scenery.
There they stood upon the plain, waving their
plume-like crown of leaves before the breeze.
You seemed to stand amid a forest of triumphal
columns. The myrtle was also found in abundance beneath the majestic palms. It is a tender
and lowly shrub, and " much resembles the saints."
It is full of fragrance, an incense worthy of Paradise; it is an evergreen, as it never withers, summer or winter. I observed also the sacred banyan,
beneath whose inviting shade thousands could as-
semble for prayer and praise. It stood in the
centre of a public garden, as a temple built by an
invisible hand, for a spiritual worship. It had a
charm for the holy soul above that of Solomon's, flaming in gold. For ages the noiseless fabric had grown,

> "a pillared shade,
> High overarched, and echoing walks between."

It was in such a cathedral that our first parents adored a present Deity. How sweet to walk in such a sanctuary when the firmament glitters like a dome of pearls, and the rays of the peaceful moon struggle through the branches, and fall quivering upon the grass beneath! In such an hour the soul may mingle with the universe, and feel as angels feel.

The appearance of the external world depends much upon the state of the soul. If melancholy brood over the mind, like a dark cloud enveloping the summit of a mountain, all nature appears in a gloomy aspect. It spreads a pall of darkness over the world. Its presence in the soul saddens the fair scene without, darkens the tints of nature's coloring, shades the flowers, and deepens the music of the winds and the waterfalls, and all the sweet voices of nature, into dirge-like strains. If the state of the soul be that of profound and unutterable peace, it throws over the objective world the mellow morning light of its own tranquillity. If the heart be joyful, it throws its sunshine upon

every thing without. It gilds the external scene
with the beams of its own delight. So to the
pure every thing is pure. The holy man walks
through society like a sunbeam through an infected
hospital, uncontaminated by the touch. God is
every where, and nature is decked with a white
robe of seraphic purity. But to the impure heart
all nature is full of uncleanness. It can see nothing but the images of its own sensuality. The
outward world shapes itself to the various mental
states of men. When the image of God is fully
restored to our fallen nature, and the soul looks
out upon the external creation through a pure
medium, then a Paradise blooms in every spot.
The grand and the beautiful, which every where
exist, become the symbolization of moral and
spiritual qualities, and of celestial realities, and
the New Jerusalem comes down from God out of
heaven, adorned as a bride for her husband. When
we reach a position of Christian experience en-
joined in the command, " Rejoice evermore," all
nature becomes vocal with praise. In the language
of Mrs. Opie,

"There seems a voice in every gale,
  A tongue in every flower,
Which tells, O Lord, the wondrous tale
  Of thy almighty power;
The birds, that rise on quivering wing,
  Proclaim their Maker's praise,
And all the mingling sounds of spring
  To thee an anthem raise.

Shall I be mute, great God, alone,
  'Midst nature's loud acclaim?
Shall not my heart, with answering tone,
  Breathe forth thy holy name?
All nature's debt is small to mine;
  Nature shall cease to be;
Thou gavest — proof of love divine —
  Immortal life to me."

At such a time the soul calls upon the outward world to join its anthem of praise, and is obeyed. Its language is, "Praise the Lord from the earth, ye dragons, and all deeps; fire and hail; snow and vapor; stormy winds fulfilling his word; mountains and all hills; fruitful trees and all cedars; beasts and all cattle; kings of the earth and all people; princes and all judges of the earth; both young men and maidens; old men and children; let them praise the name of the Lord; for his name alone is excellent, his glory is above earth and heaven." (Ps. cxlviii. 7–13.) Thus the harmony between what we call nature, and the soul, is restored. God is seen and praised every where. Man becomes the high priest of nature to direct its worship; and the inanimate world coöperates with the soul to reveal and glorify God; and the redeemed spirit is restored to its true position, at the head of all his works.

In the Happy Islands melancholy could find no home, though before reaching this restored Paradise, it sometimes haunts the soul like a spectre, and cleaves to it like the poisoned tunic of Nessus, and cannot be shaken off. The sense of loneliness is gone. The soul, united to God, the spring of all its joy, finds companionship in the pathless woods, and divine society upon the most lonely shore. In the midst of a desert at midnight, it feels a rapture inexpressible, and hears, in its deep silence, the voice of God. It can say, in the most unbroken solitude, where none intrudes, " I am not alone, for the Father is with me." In the Island of Euphrosyne melancholy never shaded the fair creations of the divine hand with her gloomy mantle. Here the sweet music of nature was never changed to the desolating howl of despair. The redeemed spirit, restored to fellowship with God, roamed over the beautiful hills, and through the delightful valleys, and along the gravelled borders of still and transparent lakes, in communion with the Holy One, and in companionship with the wise and holy. Such was the spirit's recovery of its lost purity, that it caused Nature to unfold all her charms, and the soul revelled in divine delights. Here stood the majestic oak, the lofty and graceful palm, the deep, embowering elms, and dark-green firs, and beneath them were interspersed almond trees, pomegranates, and vines; and all glowed with the presence of Divinity.

There was one thing observable in the moral condition of the people of the Happy Islands, which seemed to make their state superior to that of the original Paradise. They had learned the art of being always happy, even at times when it would seem impossible for human nature to rejoice. They had learned one thing which our first parents did not acquire in Eden. From the lofty moral position to which abounding grace had raised them, they could say, " Being justified by faith, we have peace with God through our Lord Jesus Christ ; by whom also we have access into that grace wherein we stand, and rejoice in hope of the glory of God. And not only so, but we glory in tribulations also." (Rom. v. 1–3.) It would seem but a small thing for our first parents, removed from all evil, as they were, to rejoice. But how it magnifies the grace of God, and renders illustrious the soul's redemption, when we rise above all life's evils, and joy in the God of our salvation ! This was a higher position than was occupied by Adam in Paradise.

The more holy a soul becomes, the more it will be inclined to the noble work of praise. As its redemption advances, thanksgiving will become more and more blended with its supplications, until, as it nears the celestial state, there will be a transition from special supplications to unceasing praise and perpetual jubilation. The soul catches the inspiration of the heavenly choirs, just as rivers, when they approach the ocean, begin to partake of the qualities and attributes of the great deep. Before a soul is fitted fully for the celestial state, it must learn to rejoice in the Lord, independently of all temporal things. It must find its bliss in God, and triumph in him alone; for it will soon be removed from all the things of sense, from all temporal conditions. If it would be happy then, it must be prepared for this abstraction from material and sensible things. To rejoice in the midst of the evils that assail us in a probationary state, to triumph in affliction, and to take joyfully the spoiling of our earthly goods, is one of the highest preparatives for an immaterial world, or a purely spiritual condition. Affliction of some kind becomes a necessary discipline for a heavenly state; it serves to break the strange enchantment that binds the soul to earthly objects. We must learn to say with David, "The Lord is our refuge and strength, a present help in time of trouble. Therefore will not we fear, though the earth be removed, and though the mountains be carried into the midst of the sea; though the waters thereof roar and be troubled, though the mountains shake with the swelling thereof." (Ps. xlvi. 1, 2.) His joy was wholly independent of earthly changes. It was not based upon finite things. He was too firmly anchored in God to be dragged from his moorings by the revolutions of time. The earth itself might vanish away, like the shadow of a cloud across a field, yet his heart was unmovably fixed upon its centre. Such a soul, in its weanedness from the earth, and its affinity for divine enjoyments, is prepared to enter upon the higher worship of the skies, and to regale itself with the entertainment of angels. The darker the night of trial, the sweeter will be the song of the spirit's triumph to the ear of God and all holy beings, just as music has a diviner melody when its strains float upon the midnight air. Blessed is that soul which has found God, its Maker, who alone giveth songs in the night. (Job xxxv. 10.) The apostle commands us to blend thanksgiving with supplication, when he enjoins us to "be careful for nothing, but in every thing, by prayer and supplication, *with thanksgiving*, to let our requests be made known unto God." (Phil. iv. 6.) But as the soul advances, in the triumphant progress of its redemption, to the frontier of the celestial kingdom, praise becomes the predominant element of prayer. In every thing it gives thanks. Prayer is a divine symphony made up of these four parts — thanksgiving, supplication, confession, and intercession. But in the holy soul, praise, like a lofty tenor, overpowers all the other parts, and is heard above their more feeble strains. "O for a gust of praise," said the dying Fletcher, "to fill the whole world!" In the Happy Islands a ceaseless flame of holy praise and spiritual joy, as quenchless as the fires of heaven, rose to God.

In this island, I saw delightfully realized and beautifully exemplified many passages of Scripture, such as the following: "The wilderness and solitary place shall be glad for them, and the desert shall rejoice and blossom as the rose. It shall blossom abundantly, and rejoice even with joy and singing. The glory of Lebanon shall be given unto it, the excellency of Carmel and Sharon; they shall see the glory of the Lord, and the excellency of our God. And the ransomed of the Lord shall return and come to Zion with songs and everlasting joy upon their heads; they shall obtain joy and gladness, and sorrow and sighing shall flee away." (Isa. xxxv. 1, 2, 10.) How great the triumphs of that grace which can make a *desert* rejoice, and the most desolate Sahara of earth to be vocal with songs of praise! The Psalmist also presents us with the idea of the people of God triumphing over the ills of life, and making a desert as a fruitful field. " Blessed is the man whose strength is in thee; in whose heart are the ways of them, who, passing through the valley of Baca, make it a well; the rain also filleth the pools." (Ps. lxiv. 5, 6.) Baca seems to have been a desolate valley, through which the tribes of Israel passed as they came up to Jerusalem to worship at the great national festivals. How happy is the man, says the Psalmist, whose heart is invigorated and strengthened by thee, whose joy is an influx of the bliss of the infinite Mind, derived from union with him, who travels the roads leading to Jerusalem with full bent of heart! He goes through the valley of Baca, or *weeping valley*, as it may be rendered, as full of joy as if it were cheered by fountains of water, or filled with delicious ponds. The pilgrim to the heavenly city will sometimes find his path leading through a valley of Baca, a region where earthly comforts are all blasted and withered. Happy for him if the comforts of God so delight his soul as to make it a well — a fountain gushing up from the life eternal. In Hab. iii. 17–19 we see the soul rejoicing in the absence of all earthly comforts, and cut off from all worldly supports and sources of joy. " Although the fig tree shall not blossom, neither shall fruit be in the vines ; the labor of the olive shall fail, and the fields shall yield no meat ; the flock shall be cut off from the fold, and there shall be no herd in the stalls ; yet I will rejoice in the Lord, I will joy in the God of my salvation. The Lord God is my strength, and he will make my feet like hinds' feet, and he will make me to walk upon my high places." That which a person loves will be his delight. His delights can flow from no other source than from his ruling love, the love in which he is rooted and grounded. That which we love the most, will appear delightful. It will be our heaven, which is only our idea of the supreme good. If our hearts are grounded in the love of the world, if we are swamped in material things, then our delight, such as it is, will be derived

from things earthly and sensual. If we are
grounded in the love of God, and of heavenly
things, we shall delight ourselves in the Lord, and
he will give us the desire of our hearts. We can
then say in the language of the prophet, "I will
rejoice in the Lord, I will joy in the God of my
salvation." In the absence of all earthly things,
the soul still finds its delight in the unchanging
and eternal Good, because its delight will always
be according to the nature of its love. In the
Island of Euphrosyne there grows in abundance a
species of tropical plant which most beautifully
symbolizes the state of the soul above described.
It belongs to an order of plants called aerial plants.
At first it strikes its roots downward into the soil,
like other plants, and derives from the earth its
appropriate nourishment. At length it puts forth
tendrils, which fasten upon something above it,
and its roots quit the ground. It derives no more
nourishment from the earth. All its support is
from the heavens above. Suspended above the
earth, it puts forth leaves and flowers which fill
all the adjacent region with their perfumes. So the
soul, in its hidden, interior, sanctified life, lives

14 *

and flourishes where the natural man could not
survive. Cut off from the world and all worldly
supports, and suspended by faith from the heavens,
it lives all the happier, for it sympathizes with the
delights of angels. It fulfils the command of the
apostle — " Rejoice evermore ; in every thing give
thanks. Rejoice in the Lord always; and again I
say, Rejoice." (1 Thess. v. 16, 18. Phil. iv. 4.)
He declares of his own experience, that though he
was sorrowful he was always rejoicing. His heart
was like what we are told by travellers of the
Baltic Sea, in which there are two currents, an
upper and an under, flowing in different directions. So in the heart of the apostle Paul, there
might be grief at the surface, yet in its profoundest depths there was a hidden under current of
joy, unaffected by any surface changes, which led
him at all times to praise God, both for what he
is in himself and for his wonderful works to the
children of men. Here was no constant ecstasy
of joy, but a perpetual and ineffable satisfaction in
the possession of God, and in the fact that his
will was done. A perpetual ecstasy of joy does
not belong to this earthly stage of our redemp-

tion; it can be found only on the celestial plains, where there is fulness of joy and pleasures forevermore. But in the purified heart the incense of praise continually ascends. It does not value God so much for his gifts as for the excellency of his nature. Hence, in the absence of all comforts, there remains an infinite reason for praising him. "By him, therefore, let us offer the sacrifice of praise continually, that is, the fruit of our lips, giving thanks to his name." (Heb. xiii. 15.) At times the sanctified heart, which is made the temple of an indwelling God, is caught upward to walk upon its high places, and gets a foregleam of celestial delights, like the disciples on the Mount of Transfiguration, where earth and heaven met and blended.

One characteristic feature of the scenery of the island of which we are speaking, was a lofty mountain, which rose from its centre. For a great distance up its sides it was cultivated, and vineyards and gardens were seen on terraces which surrounded it, and which appeared like wreaths of verdure encircling it. Its summit rose to a vast height, and the view from it surpassed any thing in the world. Scattered along upon its sides were

beautiful mansions, fit to be the residence of angels, adorned with every thing that could gratify
the eye, and free for any who desired to occupy them. Numerous perennial springs, clear as
crystal, and perfectly pure, gushed from its base
and its sides. These springs were always of the
same temperature every season of the year; the
quantity of water was always the same, even during the longest drought of summer. The springs,
with which I had been acquainted in other parts
of the world, were much affected by the changes
in the atmosphere or seasons. In the rainy season
they were full to overflowing; during the drought
of summer, when they were most needed, they were
either very low or else entirely dry. In the winter, instead of retaining the same temperature as
in summer, they were usually frozen up. These
springs, coming deep from the base of the mountain, were subject to no such variations. The
mountain was called Pisgah, which signifies in the
Hebrew tongue Purity, or it was sometimes called
the Mount of Transfiguration. The people of the
island occasionally ascended to its summit. This
was accomplished by no violent effort or hard labor.

The path wound round the mountain so that the ascent was easy, and it was lined on either side by fragrant shrubs in blossom. Experience had shown that when a person attempted to force himself by great efforts, such as running and leaping, he never gained any higher elevation, though he worked himself into an intense excitement. The movement of my body reminded me of the motion of the gods as described by Homer. It was neither flying nor walking, but gliding. I moved along rapidly, gently, and with ease. On reaching the summit there was found a level space of many acres, containing a Paradise, or pleasure garden, filled with flowers and fruits the whole year. The walks around this delightful place were overhung with hedges of pomegranate, myrtle, oleander, and white rose in blossom. Sometimes this lavish profusion of color and of fragrance met overhead, laced together by grape vines in bloom. The rays of the sun struggled through the roof, and, painted with the hues of the flowers, fell upon the gravelled pavement, which glittered like pearls and precious gems. How different was this from the summit of many other lofty mountains which I had

visited! Usually, as you reach their tops, you find
a region where desolation has its throne, and which
appears to be the home of the destroying angel.
You often enter the domain of everlasting winter,
where tempests forever howl. But the summit of
this mountain was different. Notwithstanding its
vast elevation, perpetual spring reigned. I stood
far above the clouds, having left the storms and
earthy vapors midway below. The rays of the sun
never fully left the summit. The evening twilight
lingered to embrace the approaching morn. From
this sublime elevation the soul gained a view of
the other shore of the ocean. So pure was the
heavenly ether, that it seemed to be near at hand.
The distant hills of the heavenly Paradise, where
angels drank immortality and joy from the smile
of a present God, were seen radiant with celestial
light. Their gilded tops were never veiled with
darkness. I gained a full view of the city of the
great King, flaming with the glory of God, and
saw the celestial plains where the redeemed walk
with God, "high in salvation and the climes of
bliss." Here the soul enjoyed a season of communion with divine things that was unutterable,

a time of abstraction from the things of sense, when the spirit was taken in a measure behind the veil, and celestial light broke in upon it. In such an hour, the soul is released from the fetters of its material inthralment, and the scenes of Paradise are unfolded to the partially unveiled spiritual senses. The soul is closed towards earth and opened towards heaven; the world and all its gilded pageantry disappears, and seraphic pleasures and ineffable delights flow into the heart. The divine influence falls upon it, like the reviving dew upon a withering flower, awaking its powers to new life and activity. At such a time, as Mr. Fletcher has observed, the soul experiences a happiness so intense as to border on misery, and be almost unendurable; for in this mortal life it can but poorly bear the force of immortal fires.

There is a certain experience of heavenly life and bliss which is symbolized by a lofty mountain. According to the correspondence which subsists between things in the natural world and the spiritual world, mountains signify a great elevation in the moral and spiritual condition of man, an elevation of the soul above the common level of its natural action to a higher plane of spiritual activity and enjoyment. Hence the ancients, who appear to have understood more clearly than the moderns the science of correspondence, built their places of worship on hills and mountains, which are called *high places* in the Scriptures. Hence Moses went up into a mountain to receive the law from God, and when he was about to die, he ascended to the summit of Pisgah, which commanded a view of the promised land. All this has its symbolical or spiritual significance as well as its literal historical meaning. When Christ would unfold the deep spirituality of the law to his followers, he went up into a mountain, and from that commanding foothold he delivered to the multitude the sermon which Matthew has recorded, which is full of the lofty utterances of divine wisdom, and in which he speaks as never man spake. Hence, when the disciples were to have a glimpse of the celestial glory, and have their spiritual senses so far uncovered as to discern the solid realities of an eternal sphere, they were taken by Christ into a high mountain, apart by themselves, where he was transfigured before them, and the heavens came down to envelop the earth with their radiance, and deluge mortality with life. Hence John, when he saw the glories of the New Jerusalem, and heaven emptying itself into earth, was transported in spirit, not in body, to a great and high mountain. The prophet Isaiah declares that in the latter days, the Messianic times, the mountain of the Lord's house, which signifies the church, shall be established in the top of the mountains, and exalted above the hills ; that is, its spiritual condition shall be greatly elevated ; it shall ascend to a higher form of divine life. It shall be exalted above its grovelling earthly state, and come into closer proximity to the heavens. It shall live a heavenly life on earth. When the time predicted by the prophet shall arrive, that the mountain of the Lord's house, or the church, shall be established in the top of the mountains, it will be an illustrious era in the history of redemption. The church will enter upon the epoch of its New Jerusalem stage of development. Heaven and earth will be brought into closer connections, and the spiritual and natural worlds will come into a more intimate conjunction. Then we shall see, as the favored disciples did, the kingdom of

God come with power, and that extraordinary vouch-safement will become the frequent experience of the children of God. At present, men, and even the church, are so buried in the things of sense, and so floundering in the dismal swamp of materialism and Sadducceism, that the celestial world is almost a *terra incognita*—an unknown land. Instead of being in living sympathy with it, it is viewed at an infinite distance, and shadows, clouds, and darkness rest upon it. But the age is coming when the two worlds will come into closer proximity, when faith will bring near the substantial realities of another sphere, and " make stirrings of deep divinity within."

Gladly would I have spent all my days in the enjoyment of such a rapturous vision of the land of the blest. I experienced what Coleridge so beautifully describes.

> " In some hour of solemn jubilee,
> The massy gates of Paradise are thrown
> Wide open, and forth come, in fragments wild,
> Sweet echoes of unearthly melodies,
> And odors snatched from beds of amaranth,
> And they that from the crystal river of life
> Spring up on freshened wing, ambrosial gales !

The favored good man in his lonely walk
Perceives them, and his silent spirit drinks
Strange bliss, which he shall recognize in heaven."

It was not thought best that the people of the Happy Islands should be all the time on the summit of this mountain. It was enough to dwell on the plains below, at the base of the mountain, among the perennial springs. The view from the mountain top served to wean the soul from earth, as did also the dark day before experienced. Ever after this, the soul was subjected to the action of two moral forces, one attracting it to the heavenly realms, where Christ dwells, the other a desire to live in order to bring the greatest possible number of mankind to share the enjoyment of its own inward blessedness. Some of the sublimest movements of the universe are produced by the action of two opposite forces, the body so situated moving in the direction of neither, but in a diagonal between them. The planets are thus moved in their orbits around their proper centres. Thus it is with the pure in heart. They are in a strait betwixt two opposite moral forces, having a desire to depart and be with Christ, which is far better, or, as

Dr. Doddridge renders the original term, better beyond all comparison and expression, and a Christ-like spirit of benevolence, which sacrifices itself to save others. Between these forces acting in opposite directions, the soul either remains in a peaceful equilibrium, or moves forward in the straight line of duty, which is a diagonal between them.

After a sufficient length of time had been spent in the enjoyment of the mountain view, I descended by the way in which I came up. The people of the islands are permitted to go to the summit of the mountain after some long inward struggle or season of internal desolation, or to prepare the soul to grapple with some fiery trial that awaits it. After this view of the heavenly glory, the thoughts and desires rise of their own accord to things above. The home centre, which is the centre of the affections, is thrown beyond earth to the immortal shores, and the soul pines for its celestial country, and longs to lose itself in the uncreated fulness of heavenly bliss. It often engages in "the soul-ravishing exercise of heavenly contemplation." It is transported on the wings of faith and hope to the heavenly sphere, and bathes its powers in uncreated light. Such a person is well described by Mr. Baxter. "As the noblest of creatures, so the noblest of Christians are they whose faces are set most direct for heaven. Such a heavenly saint, who hath been rapt up to God in his contemplations, and is newly come down from his views of Christ, — what discoveries will he make of those superior regions! How high and sacred is his discourse! Enough to convince an understanding hearer that he hath seen the Lord, and that no man could speak such words except he had been with God. This, this is the noble Christian. The most famous mountains and trees are those that reach nearest to heaven, and he is the choicest Christian whose heart is most frequently and delightfully there."

"No sickness there,
No weary wasting of the frame away,
No fearful shrinking from the midnight air,
No dread of summer's bright and fervid ray!

No hidden grief,
No wild and cheerless vision of despair,
No vain petition for a swift relief,
No tearful eye, no broken heart, are there.

Care has no home
Within that realm of ceaseless praise and song:

15 *

Its tossing billows break and melt in foam,
Far from the mansions of the spirit-throng.

The storm's black wing
Is never spread athwart celestial skies;
Its wailings blend not with the voice of Spring,
As some too tender floweret fades and dies.

No night distils
Its chilling dews upon the tender frame;
No morn is needed there: the light which fills
The land of glory, from its Maker came.

No parted friends
O'er mournful recollections have to weep;
No bed of death enduring love attends,
To watch the coming of a pulseless sleep!

No withered flower
Or blasted bud celestial gardens know!
No scorching blast, or fierce descending shower
Scatter destruction like a ruthless foe.

No battle word
Startles the sacred hosts with fear and dread!
The song of peace, creation's morning heard,
Is sung wherever angel footsteps tread.

Let us depart,
If home like this await the weary soul!
Look up, thou stricken one! thy wounded heart
Shall bleed no more at sorrow's stern control.

With faith our guide,
White-robed and innocent to tread the way,
Why fear to plunge in Jordan's rolling tide,
And find the haven of eternal day?"

CHAPTER VII.

THE ISLAND OF PLEROPHORIA.

Nature and Office of Faith. — The Attainment of Certainty in Religion. — Certainty of the divine Existence. — Three Degrees of divine Knowledge. — Illustrated by Columbus. — Elevation above the Realm of Sense. — Right Views of the divine Character an Element of an assured Faith. — Servile Fear removed. — Undoubting Credence of the Promises. — Witness of the Spirit. — The prophetic State. — No new Revelations. — Habitual Faith. — Faith sustains to Love a causal Relation. — Assurance of Hope. — Affectionate Confidence. — State of Innocence.

DURING MY stay in the Happy Islands, I visited the whole group, and passed repeatedly through the whole circle. The Island of Plerophoria, or Assurance, was often visited, and in fact was a favorite resort. Before coming to this restored Paradise, the soul is sometimes in a wilderness of doubts and fears; but here they never enter as a disturbing element in the tranquillity of the spirit. Here they walk by faith, and not by sight.

Faith is the substance of things hoped for, or, as Dr. Doddridge renders it, the *confident expectation* of those things for which we hope; it is the *evidence*, or, as some translate, " the convincing proof or demonstration," of things not seen, or those things that are not apprehensible by sensation. Its office in the mental economy is to give us a knowledge of those things that lie beyond the circle of sense. God has given to man five senses, by means of which the soul is placed in communication with the material universe, and is fitted for existence, and for the accomplishment of certain uses in this visible world. By these senses we come to the knowledge of the existence and properties of material things. But man, by virtue of his complex being, composed as he is of soul and body, combines in his structure not only earth, but heaven. As to his inmost being, he is a spirit, and stands related to a world of solid realities that lies beyond the realm of sense. Into this world of unseen realities, infinitely more important than this material and sensible world, the natural sight cannot penetrate. The senses can give us no information respecting it. By faith we are put in communication with that invisible world, and those eternal realities which it contains. In that loftier stage of faith, and that higher position of spiritual life, which is called full assurance of faith, the soul is as really in communication with the unseen world, as it is with the world of matter. It looks to those things that are unseen and eternal, as well as to things seen and temporal; and the soul just as really knows these invisible realities by faith, which is an interior sense, adapted to the cognizance of spiritual things, as it does the form and color of objects by sight. By faith the soul just as undoubtedly and really perceives the divine Being, as the eye beholds the sun in the heavens. Faith is not opposed to knowledge, for much of our knowledge is derived from no other source, but is to be distinguished from sensation. The senses act only in a limited area; but outside of this there are realities, and faith comes in where sense leaves us, and extends the boundaries of our knowledge. The knowledge of those supersensual realities derived to us by faith is as certain and reliable as from any other source. Our senses are as liable to deceive us as our faith. We are as certain of some things we never saw, as we are of any facts which have come to the cognizance of the spirit through the inlet of sensation.

In the spiritual life there is a position of faith which is the "convincing proof," or demonstration, of unseen realities. It is the attainment of *certainty* in religion. So far as belief is an element of faith, it may exist in various degrees. In its lowest stage it is what we call presumption; in a higher, probability; and in its highest degree, it becomes certainty — an undoubting credence, which is sometimes called knowledge. When the Christian spirit gets beyond the withering, desolating influence of doubt, and rests upon the unshaken rock of certainty, it rises into a higher life. The soul, by means of such a faith, is in sympathy with the celestial realms. In the language of John Rogers, the celebrated martyr of Smithfield, such persons "live by faith in the Son of God, above the letter, in the *life;* above the form, in the *power;* above self, in a higher self; so that they are no longer themselves, but are by the grace of God what they are; not doubting that they shall appear perfect in Christ's righteousness, being pardoned by his death, purged by his blood, sanctified by his Spirit, and saved by his power." (*Upham's Interior Life*, p. 58.)

The first element of that matured faith, which is denominated assurance, is the attainment of *certainty* as to the divine existence and perfections. It no more doubts these, than it does the testimony of the senses as to the existence and properties of material things. The being of God is the most *real* and certain of any thing in the universe. He is the ground of all existence, the fountain of all life. He is the only Being who has existence in himself. Every thing which has a being finds the root of its existence, and its *subsistence*, or continued existence, in the infinite Life. The life of a soul, or an insect, is a stream flowing from that Fountain; and were it not continually supplied from its Source, it would flow away and cease to be. Before we can be assured of the existence of any thing, we must reach an undoubting certainty of the existence of the great First Cause. There are three stages in the prog-

ress of a soul in the knowledge of God. The
first marks the lowest position of faith — a mere
belief, more or less strong, that God is, and that
he is every where. This belief of the existence of
the infinite One has been enstamped on the universal mind. It prevails among the most barba-
rous peoples, so that the missionary, according to
Dr. Livingstone, has not to create it by argument,
but only to appeal to it. The second stage in the
progress of the soul in the knowledge of the
Deity, is the demonstration of reason. There are
two routes, by which the intellect arrives at the
demonstration of the being of a God. By the
one, the mind infers, from the numerous marks of
intelligent and benevolent design every where dis-
coverable in the universe, the existence of an
intelligent and benevolent Contriver as the only
Cause, adequate to the known effects. The proof
rests upon the axiom, that every effect must have
a cause. Such reasoning does not originate in the
human mind the belief of a God, but demonstrates
to reason the correctness of our preconceived idea
of the divine existence. The other process by
which the intellect arrives at an undoubting per-

suasion of the fundamental truth that God exists, is by an examination of the structure of the mind itself, which is such that no one can avoid the conception of an infinitely perfect Being. It is a necessity of thought to believe in something infinite and eternal. In either of these ways the reason may be as certain that God is, as that the three angles of a triangle are equal to two right angles. The third and last stage is an *intuition* of God, an actual experience of the divine, an interior consciousness of the Deity. To illustrate these three stages of divine knowledge, take Columbus in search of a new world. There was, first, the idea or belief that such a world existed. Then he set himself to demonstrate the necessity of it, asserting, from his knowledge of the earth, that a western continent was necessary to balance the eastern. Here was the demonstration of reason. But with this alone he could not rest. He must place himself in actual contact with it. He must kneel upon it, and have a conscious experience of its reality. This last step corresponds to the highest stage of the soul in the progress of its knowledge of God. Short of an intuition or inward perception of the Deity, the human spirit never can rest. We must grasp the God we seek.

In a low degree of faith, the soul is much fettered by sense. It is in bondage to an inthralling externalism, and its perception of the divine is dimmed by a materialistic bent of mind. Like the sensuous Jews of the age of Christ, its gross mental perceptions must see signs and wonders, or it will not believe. But in the lofty stage of faith denominated by St. Paul "assurance," the soul does not depend at all upon outward signs and appearances. It does not, like Thomas, demand that the proof be brought into the sphere of sensation; but the soul goes behind the veil of sense, and is transported beyond the realm of sense. Such a faith does not arise from any thing outward, and rests not upon external signs or appearances, but upon an invisible God, of whose all-pervading life it has an inward consciousness. Blessed are they that have not seen, and yet have believed, said Christ to Peter, who in a happy moment recognized in the Son of Man the Son of God, and by a spiritual intuition perceived beneath the servant form the hidden Divinity, and was led to confess the Messiah. "Blessed art thou, Simon Barjona, for flesh and blood hath not revealed it unto thee, but my Father who is in heaven." (Matt. xvi. 16, 17.) By "flesh and blood" we may understand, not merely man, but all mere human testimony, and all outward evidence. Peter's recognition of the Godhead in Christ was a flash of divine light that broke through the sensuous envelope, which, at that time, enclosed his spiritual life. Happy is the man who can discern the divine presence independent of all outward things; who is elevated above the external world, and carried out of the sphere of sense. He finds God in the hidden depths of his soul; beholds him there, without form or parts; sees him without the intervention of any sensuous image; and knows him without even a name; that is, as something which no name can express. He is the incomprehensible Life, Light, and Love, within the sphere of whose influence the holy soul consciously floats. Such a faith brings the finite spirit within the circle in which the divine Being imparts to it himself and his own blessedness, and the soul receives the radiations of the divine life. He who attains to such an intuitive apprehension of God, and sees him who is invisible, needs no outward evidence or sensible image. How rich in heavenly blessedness are those moments when the soul, transported out of the sphere of sense, loses itself in the depths of God, yet so as to retain a consciousness of the self-subsistence of the creaturely spirit; when the infinite and finite spirits meet, and the two are made one, so that both retain all the attributes belonging to each! Such an hour of holy fellowship and celestial foretastes is worth an age of mere sense. It is then that the angelic in human nature, which is now imprisoned as a chrysalis in this material covering, begins to rend the sensuous envelope, and unfold its wings to soar amid the supersensual glories of the heavenly state.

The highest evidence of God's existence, at least to my own mind, is not derived from outward things. It is true the external world was made to reveal and glorify God, and to bring the perfections of an invisible Godhead within the grasp of the senses and the reason. These outward things, which lie in the circumference of being, constitute a thread of light, which reason may trace inward, till it arrives at the Central Life. Yet if every material thing in the universe were annihilated, and there was nothing in empty space but God and myself, there would remain the highest possible evidence that he exists. In fact the laws of our spiritual being are such that we cannot escape the conception of the absolute and infinite. The finite, which is a subject of consciousness, conducts the soul to the infinite, as necessarily and infallibly as the radius of a circle leads to the centre. They cannot be separated in our thought. If we think of space limited and finite, we must think of unlimited space, which is immensity. If we have the idea of time limited, we must conceive of time infinite, which is eternity. So of cause, of knowledge, wisdom, holiness, goodness. But if we have the idea of infinite knowledge, we cannot avoid the conception of an infinite Being, of whom it is an attribute. A quality cannot exist separate from the substance or essence in which it inheres. We cannot believe in the existence of infinite goodness separate from an infinitely good Being, any more than a ray of light

16*

can be cut off from the luminous body. Hence we have not only the abstract *idea* of infinite perfection, but of an infinite Being or Existence, whom it clothes as an atmosphere of light does the sun. Reason may here rest satisfied that there is a God; but we may go farther inward than reason itself, and in the inmost centre of our being perceive the infinite One. When, through a moral harmony subsisting between the soul and the divine nature, we are brought into an interior union with, and experience of, God, he is no longer merely an *idea* of the abstract intellect, like the God of the Grecian philosophy, but the *living* God. He is not only apprehended by reason, but *felt* in the depth of the soul, where he perpetually dwells, as the Schechinah dwelt in the most holy place of the temple. I apprehend the more spiritual a soul becomes, the more it is released from the bondage of sense, the less it will rely upon the outward world for the proof of the divine existence. The popular argument derived from the marks of design, or contrivance, every where observable in nature, and which is an argument so well adapted to a material way of thinking, will give place to a more ideal and spiritual proof.

It is an element of the state of assured faith that the soul has proper views of the nature and character of God. The words of the apostle Paul, in a mitigated sense, find here their application, and are not to be confined wholly to the immortal state. " When that which is perfect is come, then that which is in part shall be done away. When I was a child, I spake as a child, I understood as a child, I thought as a child; but when I became a man I put away childish things. For now we see through a glass darkly, but then face to face; now I know in part, but then shall I know even as also I am known." (1 Cor. xiii. 10–12.) It is important that we possess correct conceptions of the divine character. The advent of that which is perfect, or the attainment of a matured faith, clears away our infantile notions of the divine nature, as the mists of night melt away before the rising sun. If we draw a distorted picture of the Deity in our imagination, which no more resembles the true God than the shapeless images of paganism are like Jehovah who made the heavens, how can we love him? We do not then really love *him*, but a creation of our own minds. An assured faith prepares the way for a pure love, by removing from the divine character the erroneous views under which it has been apprehended. The idea of God becomes purely spiritual, and he is contemplated without the intervention of any sensuous representations. He does not truly know God who views him as possessing any of the properties of matter. A perfect faith elevates the soul above these infantile conceptions of the Divinity. It was the remark of St. Augustine, " that the capacity of the soul is such as to enable it to have ideas independently of the direct action of the senses ; and which therefore represent things that are not characterized by extension and form, and any other attributes that are visible and tangible." This means simply that the human spirit may contemplate purely spiritual things, and is all included in St. Paul's definition of faith, as the demonstration of unseen realities, or of things that lie beyond the contracted boundaries of sense. It does not view God as seated in the third heavens, subject to the finite limitations of time and space, but feels that there is not a point in unbounded space where the whole undivided God is not, and at every point the soul may be put in communication with the whole Deity. Such a faith finds him in all the operations of nature. In that respect it makes no distinction between a miracle and an event occurring in the ordinary course of things. In the germination of a grain of wheat it sees a divine power, as well as in the resurrection of Lazarus. It recognizes the divine agency in the rise of an empire and in the fall of a sparrow. It raises every event to the dignity of a providence. The laws of nature become to such a faith only the uniform mode in which a divine power acts. It sees in Christ a God, and that God in every page of the world's annals, and in every event that befalls us. Perhaps few rise to this higher knowledge of God. Few become free from the bondage of sense, and live in the region of pure faith. Those powers of our complex nature that unite us to the external creation have an undue predominance over our spiritual being, which links us to celestial things. Few rise wholly out of those puerile notions of the divine nature which float before the mind of childhood. As childhood discerns in human nature but little that is not material, so it sees in God nothing but its idea of humanity projected into the heavens. Yet it is better to know God through the senses, than not at all. This elementary and imperfect knowledge may constitute the basis of that which is spiritual. It is better to see him as something visible and tangible to the senses, as he dwelt in the midst of ancient Israel, than never to behold him at all. Yet there is a more exalted stage of divine knowledge. Under the gospel, which has cleared away the incrustation of sense from the idea of God, we may attain as pure a knowledge of him as was possessed by Adam in Paradise. When the redeemed spirit arrives to the maturity of Christian manhood, it puts away childish things. But it is the law of the soul's development in this temporal stadium of its progress, that there should be first that which is earthy, then that which is heavenly. Its sensualism, with which it begins existence, gives place to a refined idealism. The mind becomes spiritualized in every department of its activity, to prepare it for a celestial flight, when it shall be fully emancipated from the limitations of time and sense.

A matured faith prepares the soul for the habitation of a pure love, by banishing from it all servile and tormenting fears of God. It presents him to the soul as the most perfect and lovely Being in the universe, more willing to impart himself to his creatures than they are to receive him. How well does Mr. Baxter say, in his directions how to live on earth a heavenly life, " Ever keep thy soul possessed with believing thoughts of the infinite love of God. Few so vile but will love those who love them. No doubt it is the death of our heavenly life to have hard thoughts of God, to conceive of him as one who would rather damn than save us. This is to put the blessed God into the similitude of Satan. When our ignorance and unbelief have drawn the most deformed picture of him in our imaginations, then we complain that we cannot love him, or delight in him. This is the case with many thousand Christians. Alas, that we should thus blaspheme God, and blast our joys! Scripture assures us that God is love, (1 John iv. 16,) that fury is not in him, (Isa. xxvii. 4,) that he hath no pleasure in the death of the wicked, but that the wicked turn from his way and live. (Ezek. xxxiii. 11.) Much more hath he testified his love to his chosen, and his full resolution effectually to save them. O that we could always think of God as we do of a friend! as of one that unfeignedly loves us, even more than we do ourselves; whose very heart is set upon us to do us good, and hath therefore provided for us an everlasting dwelling with himself!" The assurance of faith removes the spirit of bondage to fear, and restores to the soul the spirit of adoption. It displaces all jealous thoughts of God, since we no longer look to him through the distorting medium of conscious guilt, but through a pure love. And perfect love becomes the best school in which to learn what God is. It is only by loving him that we come *really* to know him. "He that loveth not, knoweth not God, for God is love." (1 John iv. 8.) A guilty soul can see in God only an object of fear. Peter, in his impulsive nature, when the divinity of Christ flashed out in the miracle of the draught of fishes, and which called into activity his slumbering consciousness of sin, felt repelled from Christ, the most lovely being in the universe. He exclaims, " Depart from me, O Lord, for I am a sinful man." At another time, under the attractive force of love, when he was invited by Christ to go away, his heart spontaneously answers, "To whom shall we go; thou hast the words of eternal life." Love conjoins the soul to its Source, but fear repels. When the soul, borne up by a mature faith, rises from the earthly to the heavenly in the knowledge of God, and loves him as he is, and for what he is, how seraphic is the flame! It is as pure as ever glowed in Eden. It is the recovery of the soul to that state of faith in which it was created. "This is the true God and eternal life. Little children, keep yourselves from idols." (1 John v. 21.)

In the state called full assurance of faith, there is not only an exemption from all doubt of the divine existence and perfections, but this certainty is transferred to all the objects of faith. The soul not only believes without the shadow of a doubt that God is, but that he is also the rewarder of them that diligently seek him. Such a person staggers not at the promise of God, but is just as certain that God will, and does, fulfil his promises as that he exists. The true knowledge of the divine perfections which he has gained furnishes an impossibility in the way of the non-fulfilment of the divine word. God is not only true, but is Truth itself; and every word which emanates from him partakes of this quality of the divine mind, and can be nothing but truth. It is a ray of the eternal Light. The promises of God, being an emanation of his character, and resting on the immutable basis of the divine veracity, cannot fail of accomplishment. To an assured faith, a blessing promised is as good as a blessing possessed. The soul in such a state reposes with the same undoubting confidence in the promises of God as it does in the uniformity of the operations of nature's laws. To believe in this uniformity of nature's laws is inherent in the essence of humanity. The man who sees the sun sink below the western horizon as much expects that it will rise again in the east, as that the universe will exist at all. He is firmly persuaded, because it is a part of his mental constitution, that there will be the same uniformity in the succession of day and night, summer and winter, seed time and harvest. So an assured faith gives the soul the same unshaken conviction of the accomplishment of the divine word, for the laws of nature and the promises of the gospel proceed from the same source — the infinite Mind. And there is, if possible, more reason to believe that the will of God will act with unvaried certainty and uniformity in fulfilling the promises of the covenant of grace, than that it will continue to act with uninterrupted regularity in nature.

The assurance of faith removes all distressing doubts of our personal acceptance with God, and adoption into the celestial family. In the Happy Islands the complaining moan, "When shall I make these gloomy doubts remove?" is never heard. Having reached an undoubting consciousness of God, and his boundless and everlasting love, they enjoy the constant, abiding witness of the Spirit that they are the children of God. In that intimate union and fellowship with God which they have reached, the secret of their pardon flows from the mind of God into their own, through the medium of the Holy Ghost. Because they are sons, God sends forth the Spirit of his Son into

their hearts, crying, Abba, Father. (Gal. iv. 6.)
They have not received the spirit that is of the
world, for that is not cognizant of divine things,
but the Spirit that is of God, that they may know
the things that are freely given to them of God;
and the Spirit itself beareth witness with their
spirit that they are the children of God. (1 Cor.
ii. 12. Rom. viii. 15, 16.) Here we observe that
the fact of our pardon and adoption is imparted
to our consciousness by the direct contact of the
Spirit of God. Some have confined the state of
assured faith to this internal divine conviction of
our sonship; but it differs from it as a part does
from the whole. It is only one element in that
moral condition we call assurance. But until the
conviction is inwrought into our inmost being, by
the Spirit of God, that we are justified from all
things through Christ, we can make no advancement in our spiritual progress. There can be no
joy or peace. In the presence of doubts and fears
of our personal adoption, our Christian graces wither
like flowers before the touch of a winter's blast.
Arvid Gradin, a pious Moravian, beautifully described to Mr. Wesley the serene blessedness ac-

companying the Plerophoria, or Full Assurance of Faith. It is, "*Requies in sanguine Christi*, &c.,—Repose in the blood of Christ,—a firm confidence in God, and persuasion of his favor; a serene peace and steadfast tranquillity of mind, with a deliverance from every fleshly desire, and from every outward and inward sin. In a word, my heart, which before was tossed like a troubled sea, was still and quiet, and in a sweet calm."

This interior communication of the soul of man with the Spirit of God, which takes place in the witness of our sonship, appears to me to be the same in its essence as the prophetic state, one of those spiritual conditions which passed from Paradise into Patriarchism, thence into Judaism, and has been carried forward into Christianity. It has often appeared to me that the religion of the gospel contains in it a concentration of all that was truly good in all previous religions. The scattered rays of good that proceeded forth from the Deity in all other systems, find now their glowing focus in Christianity. In Judaism especially, there were many things of permanent excellence, many germs of an undecaying good, which were gathered up by Christ, and .transplanted in the gospel age, to be more perfectly developed in a better soil, and under a brighter sun. On the dissolution of the old world, there were some things of enduring excellence that were not to vanish away. Every thing of real value in all preceding dispensations has passed down into Christianity, and there become the property of all true believers. For it is a characteristic feature of Christianity to render common and universal what was in Judaism the privilege of only a few. That which might be deemed an extraordinary vouchsafement of the Deity may now be the ordinary experience of believers. See this illustrated in the universal priestly character of Christians. The privilege of entering the most holy place, enjoyed only by the high priest, and that but once a year, is now given, according to St. Paul, to all the children of God, and every day and hour of their lives. By a new and living way, because of its more spiritual character, they may pass beyond the veil into the holiest place of all. So that the priestly aristocracy has disappeared from the church, and given place to the universal priestly dignity of the followers of Christ.

Every believer is not only now a priest, but a high priest, and all the pontifical functions are discharged by him. The holy days, and particular times and seasons, are extended by Christ to the whole life. The unapproachable sanctity of particular places, as the temple, is now extended to every point of the earth's surface, where the soul holds communion with a present God. In every place, hallowed by the presence of Deity, we are to lift up holy hands without wrath and doubting. So with regard to the prophetic state. It gleams as a vein of pure gold amid the dross of the worthless externalism of the former age. It was not to vanish away on the dissolving of the Jewish heavens, but is among those priceless goods which cannot be shaken, and which contain an immortal germ. When Moses was informed that Eldad and Medad were prophesying in the camp, he uttered the wish that in an after age proved prophetic— "Would God that all the Lord's people were prophets, and that the Lord would put his Spirit upon them." (Num. xi. 29.) This benevolent wish has, by the universal love of God, been made a living reality by the gospel. The measure of the

Spirit's influence, which was necessary to constitute the prophetic state, is not now confined to the few. This once extraordinary vouchsafement has now become the common experience of the pure in heart. The prophet Joel broke the announcement to his incredulous countrymen, that in the last days, the Messianic age, it should come to pass that Jehovah would pour out his Spirit upon all flesh, and their sons and their daughters should prophesy. (Joel ii. 28.) This was fulfilled on the opening of the Christian age on the day of Pentecost. From that time, heaven has poured itself more largely and universally into the mind of God's people. The Spirit's influence, which prophets only enjoyed in the patriarchal and Mosaic church, is now the privilege of all. The prophetic state is no longer confined to the few, and is not a peculiarity of Judaism. Does not Christianity bring the soul into as close a fellowship with God as Judaism did? Is God less familiar with the Christian than he was with the Jew? In this respect he that is least in the kingdom of heaven is greater than John the Baptist. But what was the essence of the prophetic state? It was not the prescience of future events. To anticipate history, to cast a piercing glance into futurity, and foretell what shall befall a nation or individual, was not the main part of prophecy, but something accidental rather than essential. There can be prophecy without predictions. But the prophetic state consisted mainly in an unclouded consciousness of God, who inly spake to the soul. The senses were called off from outward objects, the soul retired into its inner sanctuary, the holy of holies, and held converse with God. All other voices were silenced, the clamor of unsatisfied desires and selfish passions ceased, the whole universe was dumb, and God's voice was heard in the depth of the spirit. This holy converse with Deity was enjoyed by Adam in Paradise, as also by Abraham and other holy patriarchs. The Jewish prophets, that succession of unworldly men, heard the voice of God within. But the same intuition of God which they enjoyed, and the same blessedness of divine internal converse, is now the privilege of all the pure in heart. God still speaks to holy souls. He speaks through the ordinary laws of mental action; in

the decisions of a sanctified judgment; in an illuminated reason; in the voice of an enlightened
conscience; and by impressing directly our consciousness. A prophet, in the New Testament
sense, is one who is taught of God, and who
speaks to others from an inward divine impulse
and conviction. When the Jewish prophet declared
of the Christian age, that all its children should
be taught of God, and that great should be their
peace, he intimates the universality of the prophetic state. What we call the witness of the
Spirit to our adoption, is the voice of God within,
not conveyed to the soul by words either external
or internal, but by impressing the inmost springs
of thought, and creating an inward consciousness
by his Holy Spirit, that we are his children. It
is in its essence the same as the prophetic state.

In the Happy Islands all are priests and prophets. But they have no new revelations. As the
system of revealed truth stands out in all its com-
pleteness, with nothing redundant, nothing defective, we are not to look for any new communica-
tions of truth from God. If God speaks, it is
generally in the language of the written word,

and always in perfect harmony with it. The Spirit may call all things to our remembrance which Christ has spoken, and apply those truths to our hearts, when the occasion demands it, with all the freshness of a new communication from heaven. There may be, and there will no doubt be, a progressive development of those germs of truth which Christ by the gospel has deposited in the mind of the race. Under the influence of the Paraclete, or divine Teacher and Comforter, the simplest sentence that ever fell from the lips of the Son of God, may be unfolded to infinity. Every sentence of the gospel, coming deep from the abyss of the divine Mind, has in it the germ of an endless expansion. The Christian mind has as yet only stirred the surface of the great deep of truth with which the gospel has flooded the world. Eternity alone can penetrate the bottom. While the holy soul, in stillness and silence, in the sacred solitude of the closet, may still hear the small voice within, in the sweetest, divinest of all harmonies, no new announcements will break upon the enraptured ear. The book is already full and crowded with truth; it is the function of prophecy to break the seven seals, and unroll the volume. Christ has not left us in orphanage. He is still with his disciples. In the deepest solitude, the holy soul is not alone. The purified heart can never be companionless. What a familiarity it has with Divinity, when assurance takes the place of its doubts, and perfect love that of its servile fear. There are no two beings in the universe who converse oftener or more familiarly than God and such a soul. Though outside of the geographical boundaries of the original Paradise, the redeemed spirit walks with God. This sweet familiarity with the Deity, which is the fruit of an assured faith, removes all doubts of our adoption into the heavenly family.

In the state of assurance, faith becomes habitual. It is no longer an effort to believe and trust, but is a spontaneity. A mental act often repeated creates a tendency in the soul to act in that direction. This law of habit applies to faith.

A mature faith is a fixed state of the will. It is not periodical, but is a ceaseless current of the soul's divine life. When faith becomes a habit and a life, it secures to the soul a constant flow of the blessings of the new covenant. Not because it has merit to purchase the divine favor, but because it renders the heart *receptive* of the blessings of grace. It brings the soul into that only condition in which it is possible for it to receive the blessings of God. It is, for instance, only by faith that the objective reconciliation to God, which Christ has wrought for us, becomes subjective, or an internal state of mind, and is appropriated to the soul's comfort. In the state of assurance, it has become a mental habit to rely upon the blood of sprinkling for acceptance with the Father. To trust in Christ alone for salvation, has become incorporated into the soul's texture, and made a part of itself. That which was once a labor, an effort of will, is now spontaneous. By this unwavering faith in the sacrifice of the cross, it is justified freely and fully. It is made as free from guilt as Adam was in Paradise. "There is, therefore, now no condemnation to them that are in Christ Jesus." (Rom. viii. 1.) The mountain of guilt and despair is upheaved from our condition. The justification of the believing soul through faith is as perfect as was the justification of our first parents by the covenant of works. Behold in this another element of the paradisiacal state restored. God forgives and forgets. "He will subdue our iniquities, and cast all our sins into the depths of the sea." (Micah vii. 19.) He pardons and restores. The soul, thus freed from all consciousness of guilt, and experiencing the blessedness of him whose iniquity is covered, and to whom the Lord will not impute sin, draws near to God in affectionate reliance. It reposes in him. It confides in him as undoubtingly as the infant rests upon the maternal bosom. Here faith, by an insensible gradation, passes into love. Such a faith is the groundwork of love. It is the very substance of love. It connects the sundered tie between God and the human spirit. It conjoins the Infinite and the finite, the Creator and the creature. It restores the soul to God, from whom it had been disjoined by the revolt of its free will. This faith sustains to love a causal relation. Such are the laws of our spiritual nature that love can be restored to our lapsed humanity only through faith. When the soul, with child-like simplicity, trusts all to God, as Adam did in Eden, then there arises in the soul the love of Paradise. The redeemed soul is like a tree planted in the courts of the Lord's palace. Faith is its vital root, love the trunk, and the graces which adorn and constitute the Christian character are the branches. If the root withers, the tree fades.

The assurance of faith removes all painful doubts respecting the soul's future blessedness, and gives it the full assurance of hope. (Heb. vi. 11.) In its habitual faith, which has caused the soul to be rooted and grounded in love, it finds a pledge of its perseverance. In its confirmed holiness, it has the beginnings and earnest of the life eternal, and is fully persuaded that it shall reach the celestial world. The apostle Paul speaks in the language of an assured hope, when he says, " We know that if our earthly house of this tabernacle were dissolved, we have a building of God, a house not made with hands, eternal in the heavens." (2 Cor. v. 1.)

> "The glorious crown of righteousness
>   To me reached out I view;
> Conqueror through him, I soon shall seize,
>   And wear it as my due."

An assured faith brings heaven near to the soul, and into the soul, and thus becomes "the substance of things hoped for." Heaven is nearer to a soul in union with God than the soul is to the body. For the human spirit is not removed from heaven so much by distance of space, or physical position, as by condition of state. It is said of the man Jesus, that he was in heaven when he was on earth. "Even the Son of man who is in heaven." Whatever was predicated of Christ's humanity may, in a mitigated sense, be asserted of every real Christian, for it is the glory of the disciple that he is like the Master. And the Christian, according to the foreknowledge of God, has been predestinated to be conformed to the image of the Son. As Christ lived and moved in the very element of heaven, so does a truly Christian soul. The heavenly heart finds in its sweet fruition of the divine presence the prophecy of its full beatitude in the immortal state; and having access into that grace wherein we stand, it rejoices in full hope of the glory of God.

There is a faith which belonged to man's primitive state of innocence; and which it will retain

in its transition to immortality, which I found restored in the Happy Islands. This faith is not
merely a reliance upon the atonement for salvation, but a state of affectionate confidence which
the soul feels towards God. All servile fear is
banished ; the redeemed spirit reclines on the
bosom of the God of love, and is not repulsed.
No sooner did man sin, than a sense of guilt came
in between the soul and its Maker. It became
jealous of God, confidence was destroyed, and man
fled away to hide himself from the divine presence. In Christ and Christianity this original
confidence is restored. The purified heart no
longer flees from God, but yields to the current
of the divine attraction, and runs to his open
arms. This affectionate confidence is the groundwork of that moral condition we call innocence,
which was man's original state, and which is the
ultimate goal of the soul's redemptive progress in
this earthly sphere. It is the highest spiritual
condition attainable by human nature, and is that
which links the soul to the consummate blessedness of the celestial realms. It is the most lovely
feature in the condition of little children, though

18 *

it exists in them more as a negative than as a
positive state. As a moral condition, it is a freedom from all evil intentions; a harmlessness of
character, based on perfect love; a freedom from
conscious guilt, which has been washed away by
the blood of Christ; a pure simplicity of heart,
exemption from all suspicion of God, and an un-
stained moral purity. When this primitive confidence is restored to the soul, how sweet is its
intercourse with Divinity! Its profound contentment in God leaves it nothing to ask; its innocence removes all its fear. In the Happy Islands
how often did the Deity come down and walk
with the redeemed race who there dwelt, in the
cool of the day! The purified soul in this state
of restored confidence and child-like innocence feels
an ineffable satisfaction in being in the presence
of God,

> "Within his circling arms to lie,
> Beset on every side."

It is difficult for the soul to come down from
that elevated position of spiritual life to which an
assured faith sometimes raises it, and from its
seraphic communion with its heavenly Friend, and

reproduce its experience in words. There is an infantile stage of Christian life, a position of weakness and instability, when we are afraid that our words express too much. There is another experience of divine things, which no language, not even the highest form of poetry, which borders upon inspiration, can express. How, then, can we describe that child-like trust and loving confidence, which man, in his pristine innocence, felt towards God, and which is restored to the pure in heart? No man in modern ecclesiastical history knew better what it was than Archbishop Fenelon. As he describes it, his language glows with the radiance of Paradise. He says, "We are with God as with a friend. At first we have a thousand things to say to our friend, and a thousand to ask of him; but, in time, all this matter of conversation is drained, and yet the pleasure of the intercourse cannot cease. We have said all; but without speaking, we take pleasure to be together, to see each other, to repose ourselves in the satisfactions of a sweet and pure friendship. We are silent, but in the silence we hear and understand each other. We know ourselves to be alike in every thing, and that our two hearts make but one; the one pours itself forth continually into the other." Such is the mutual communication between God and the holy heart. This silent communion is only faintly imaged by the union of two earthly friends, and their sweet but silent intercourse of looks and smiles. Here is no coyness, no shyness, no reserve, no distance, but an ineffable oneness of spirit. This confidence hath great recompense of reward. It is this that made Abraham the intimate friend and bosom confidant of Jehovah. This familiar, confiding repose in the love of God is a faith which abideth forever. It is a spark of the immortal life. "Now abideth faith, hope, charity, these three; but the greatest of these is charity." (1 Cor. xiii. 13.) This endearing confidence the soul carries with it in its ascent into the heavenly life. There it brings the hallowed spirit near to God, to spend an endless age in the sweet endearments of his love, which shall perpetually "twine around the soul." This restored confidence is often referred to in the Scriptures, and as belonging to this temporal stage of our redemption. "In whom [Christ] we have boldness, and access with confidence, by the faith of him." (Eph. iii. 12.) Here is described a confident trust, a freedom from an unbelieving timidity, which characterizes the intercourse of the Christian spirit with God. Says the apostle John, who furnishes the best example of this degree of faith, "And now, little children, abide in him, that when he shall appear, we may have confidence, and not be ashamed before him at his coming." (1 John ii. 28.) "Beloved, if our heart condemn us not, then have we confidence toward God." (1 John iii. 21.) Again, "This is the confidence that we have in him, that if we ask any thing according to his will, he heareth us." (1 John v. 14.) The soul united to Christ by a vital faith feels no condemnation, but a sweet persuasion of divine acceptance, an inward assurance that God is well pleased. This inward conviction of God's everlasting love to us becomes so deeply seated in our consciousness, that no darkness or trouble can destroy it. Its language is, " For I am persuaded, that neither death, nor life, nor angels, nor principalities, nor powers, nor things present, nor things to come, nor height, nor depth, nor any other creature, shall be able to separate us from the love of God which is in Christ Jesus our Lord." (Rom. viii. 38, 39.) Thus "the work of righteousness shall be peace, and the effect of righteousness, quietness and assurance forever." (Isa. xxxii. 17.) "Having therefore, brethren, boldness [or liberty, permission] to enter into the holiest by the blood of Jesus, by a new and living way, which he hath consecrated for us, through the vail, that is to say, his flesh; and having a high priest over the house of God; let us draw near with a true heart, in full assurance of faith, having our hearts sprinkled from an evil conscience, and our bodies washed with pure water." (Heb. x. 19–22.)

CHAPTER VIII.

TELEIA AGAPE, OR THE REALM OF PURE LOVE.

*Earth joined to Heaven. — The Bride's Chamber. — Friendship
with Jesus. — Excellency of Love. — What is perfect Love?
It is sincere Love; it is perpetual; a fixed state of the
will; it is supreme. — Grateful Love. — Loving God alone.
— Ceaseless Prayer. — The Love of God for his own Sake. —
Quotation from Abelard. — It casts out Fear. — The Cure of
wandering Thoughts. — Spontaneous Obedience. — Love a
powerful Principle. — Love restored in the Happy Islands. —
The lost Harmony of the outward World. — State of Society. —
Longevity of the People. — Death abolished. — Correspondence
of the material World with the spiritual.*

FROM THE Island of Plerophoria I passed
over into Teleia Agape, or the realm of Pure
Love. In no island of the whole group did I
trace more of the lineaments of Paradise than
here. The yearnings of the soul for earth's lost
garden of delights were here more fully satisfied
than ever they before had been. Here I found a

people who had begun to wear the garments of
eternal day, and the island seemed to be on the
confines of the earthly state, where it borders upon
the celestial realms, and the spirit finds itself in
the antechamber of heaven. As the portico of
Solomon's Temple was adorned with goodly gifts,
such as a golden vine of immense value, so in
this island the sanctified spirit enjoyed a foretaste
of a heavenly repast, and partook of angels' food.
The inhabitants could truly say, —

> "I hold a middle rank 'twixt heaven and earth,
> On the last verge of mortal being stand,
> Close to the realms where angels have their birth,
> Just on the boundaries of the spirit land."

Through a divine sympathy of spirit, the people
of the celestial plains seemed to be brought near,
and heaven appeared to be in the immediate neighborhood. The soul here could pass over the abyss
that separates the two worlds, and which faith
had bridged, and, on the wings of love, soar to its
divine Source and Author. The love which here
reigned seemed to bind the whole universe of holy
beings in one bundle of life. By virtue of his
internal spiritual nature, which had been cleansed

and filled with holy love, man here seemed an inhabitant of the spiritual world, while at the same time, in consequence of his external material covering, he dwelt in the natural world. Thus he is an inhabitant of both worlds, and finds in his complex being adaptations to each, just as certain animal existences have been observed in a transition state from the element in which they had their birth to a higher condition of life, and have organs that belong to each. He who loves God supremely and perfectly is not only in communion with all the saints on earth, but is in the communion of the angels of heaven; and like the holy apostle, he "bows his knees before the Father of our Lord Jesus Christ, of whom the whole family in heaven and earth is named." (Eph. iii. 14, 15.) The common love of God constitutes a sympathetic bond, a fellow-feeling, which brings them near, for we are not separated from the heavenly branch of the Lord's family by spatial distances, so much as by a disagreement of spiritual state. This chasm perfect love had filled in the Happy Islands, and through these blissful groves angels unseen delighted to wander. It is thought by some philosophers that the eastern and western hemispheres were once together, and by some violent disruption of nature were sundered. The prominences of the one continent seem now ready to fit into the depressions of the other, if they could only be brought together again. So the celestial and earthly worlds, like the two continents, were once together. Sin caused a violent disruption of the two, but perfect love being restored to the whole of earth, the two worlds would again flow together.

In the island which I had now entered was found the bride's chamber, where she made ready for the bridegroom. "The King's daughter, the church, is here all glorious within; her clothing is of wrought gold. She shall be brought unto the King in raiment of needlework; and the virgins, her companions that follow her, shall be brought unto him. With gladness and rejoicing shall they be brought; they shall enter into the King's palace." (Ps. xlv. 13–15.) Here the wedding garment was put on, and the heart often exclaimed, "I will greatly rejoice in the Lord; my soul shall be joyful in my God; for he hath clothed me with the garments of salvation, he hath covered me with the robe of righteousness, as a bridegroom decketh himself with ornaments, and as a bride adorneth herself with her jewels." (Isa. lxi. 10.) The soul also hears the voice of God, saying, " I will betroth thee unto me forever ; yea, I will betroth thee unto me in righteousness, and in judgment, and in loving kindness, and in mercies. I will even betroth thee unto me in faithfulness." (Hosea ii. 19, 20.)

There is an intimate union with Christ, a mutual love and friendship, which may, with propriety, be called the espousal of the soul to Christ, because it is the realization of what is symbolized by the divine institution of marriage, which, according to St. Paul, has its spiritual significance. (Eph. v. 32.) Marriage, in its essence, is a union of two souls in one through love. The founder of the Peripatetic philosophy has defined friendship to be "one soul in two bodies." There is such a friendship with Jesus. He says to his disciples, " Ye are no longer servants, but friends, for the servant knoweth not what his lord doeth." When the soul rises above that spiritual condition symbolized by a servant, and rises to that of a confidant of Jesus, he unbosoms himself to that soul in the endearments of the most familiar intercourse. This friendship is based upon a similarity of character and affinity of disposition. Where this is wanting there can be no permanent and perfect union. There will be more points of repulsion than attraction, and a sense of distance will be the result. The holy friendship existing between the Lord and his sanctified people is based on a sympathy of feeling and temper, which becomes perpetually stronger by the fellowship to which the soul is admitted. For one always carries about with him the impress of his nearest friends. He receives into his inner life their modes of thought and expression, their feelings, their likes and dislikes. Could we look into the heart of the real Christian through the separating veil, we should see there the image of Jesus. He is joined to the Lord, and is one spirit with him. The friendships of the world, such as commercial friendships, and such as appear to exist between bad men engaged in the same employment, as thieves and pirates, are based upon the lower and selfish sentiments of our nature, and are mere temporary attachments springing from interest, and may suddenly cease, or change to deadly enmity and rancor. The friendship the redeemed spirit has with Jesus is founded upon the holiest sentiments and principles of our nature, and is more lasting than Ararat or the Andes. Flowing from the purest source, it will outlive the pyramids, survive the conflagration of the world, and exist through the revolving cycles of eternal ages. It will forever glow in the fadeless splendors of an immortal day. The voice of God is, "I will betroth thee unto me forever."

In this island I had entered the domain of pure love and the realm of peace. Love is the principle of holiness, and the highest bliss of the soul. The heaven of heavens is love. The power to love God is the greatest gift bestowed upon human nature. It is the crowning blessing of infinite goodness. He who loves nothing but himself is in the profoundest misery. It is the very essence of hell. To love any thing out of ourselves makes the soul happier. But to love Jesus, and be conscious that he loves us, is to experience the holiest and happiest emotion of the human heart. O the bliss, the heavenly sweetness, of that hour when

19 *

God alone is loved! It is heaven come down to earth. It is Paradise repaired. A soul consumed with the love of God and of Christ droops in the absence of God, or if he but conceal his face, like a flower smitten with an autumnal frost. Where perfect love reigns, the soul cleaves to Jesus. The thought of separation is a pang of agony. Life without him would be a burden, and the universe a gloomy solitude. The highest ideal of heavenly bliss is an eternal union with him — to be where he is and to be like him. When he is present, all is well; pain is sweet, labor is rest, and death itself, as the messenger to summon and conduct us to his presence on high, is welcome. When he is absent, a vacuum is left which the whole universe cannot fill. All comfort withers and dies. The least adversity or cross is insupportable.

He who loves God according to the measure of his capacity is as happy as his nature will admit. It is the same bliss as Eden afforded. "It is," says Jeremy Taylor, "the image and little representation of heaven; it is beatitude in picture, or rather the infancy and beginnings of glory." In Paradise, where Adam dwelt in innocence and peace, this was the supreme law—" Thou shalt love the Lord thy God with all thy heart, and with all thy soul, and with all thy mind, and with all thy strength, and thy neighbor as thyself." This law he perfectly kept. In the Happy Islands it was put into their minds and written on their hearts, and implanted so deep within that it could not be easily effaced. With the restoration of this law, and its perfect observance by the redeemed race who there dwelt, came back the holiness and the consequent bliss of Paradise. This is the old commandment, and the new commandment, and the sum of all the divine commandments. It is the whole law and the prophets. It reduces to its ultimate analysis the whole duty of all moral intelligences. It is love alone that can give value to faith, and all outward deeds and observances. Without it they are worthless. (1 Cor. xiii. 1–3.) All other Christian graces are only different forms of love. Under proper circumstances, and at a fitting opportunity, it becomes patience, or meekness, or chastity, or temperance, or humility, or self-denial, or zeal. It is the soul of every virtue, the substratum of every moral excellence. Every holy temper, or disposition, or rewardable act of obedience, among angels or men, is an outgrowth from this root. He who loves *what* he ought, and in the proper *degree*, will be right and acceptable to God in every thing else. Against such there is no law. Sinai itself is satisfied and approves. It is the band of perfection, and the fulfilling of the law.

What is that *perfect* love which reigned in Paradise, and which Christ brought to earth again from heaven, whither it had fled? For as Socrates brought philosophy from heaven to dwell with men, so Christ brought not only a celestial philosophy to earth, but deposited in the souls of his disciples a celestial love, which has dwelt familiarly with them ever since. Perfect love is sincere love, true love, love from the bottom of the heart. Dissembled love is like painted fire, which is only a flame in appearance. Perfect love is lodged in the inmost centre of the heart, below all other loves. It is perpetual and constant. It is not like an intermittent spring, sometimes overflowing, and then its waters sinking out of sight; it does not come and go like the tide, but ever flows onward like a majestic river. If it should cease for a moment, it would not be perfect. It is like the holy fire of the temple which the priest kept continually burning. It is not characterized by violence, like a passion, but is a pure and tranquil principle. It is not merely an emotion, but a fixed state of the will. It may, and often does, rise into a rapturous emotion, a seraphic flame, but may exist not as an emotional state, but as a settled bent of the will. Emotions are as variable as the inconstant winds; pure love is as fixed as the poles of the earth, or the pillars of heaven. A child may love his father, or a parent may love his son, when he is not even thinking of him. Other thoughts fill his mind, other cares occupy his whole attention. Yet love never ceases for a moment. As soon as the thought of the endeared object gains admittance, then love is felt. Before, it existed as a state of the will, ready to rise into an emotion when occasion permitted. The highest degree of love carries the will with it, and may exist without feeling, just as the highest degree of faith is knowing without seeing.

In the Happy Islands there reigned *supreme* love.

If there be in the universe any thing which we love as much or more than God, any thing we more highly prize, our love is defective, and we have seen an end of its perfection. In a qualified sense, perfect love is loving God alone. All other love is so small in comparison, so feeble in degree, as to seem nothing. The love of God has swallowed up all other love. Every thing else is loved in him, and for his sake. In Paradise man loved every thing that was morally beautiful and excellent, and which was a ray from God; yet the love which Adam bore to his Maker was above all. St. Paul stands forth as the representative of all the pure in heart when he says, "Yea, I count all things but loss for the excellency of the knowledge of Christ Jesus my Lord." (Phil. iii. 8.) Such a love *gives* all, to find all again in God.

Perfect love is grateful love. It is the most acceptable gift we can offer in return for the unnumbered blessings of Providence and grace. The soul where pure love reigns goes forth in thankfulness to its divine Benefactor for all his mercies, for all those precious emanations from him which we have enjoyed. It loves him for his amazing goodness to us. It traces every good an perfect gift back to the Father of lights. In him it finds the fountain of life, of power, of wisdom, and of bliss, and the more it values the gifts, the more it loves the Giver. This gratitude, though it has reference to the gifts of God to us, is not selfish. As Mr. Hervey has said, "There is something in it noble, disinterested, and generously devout." It existed in Paradise when man came pure from the hand of his Maker; it will be perpetuated in heaven, where God is all and in all, and where it glows in the whole angelic mind, and bursts forth in anthems of loftiest praise. Grateful love in the perfected heart becomes ceaseless praise. Just as the distant waterfall, in the silence of the night, continually murmurs its song to the stars above, so the ear of God forever hears the low breathings of grateful praise proceeding from the heart where perfect love reigns. This form of love ought to be stronger in the Christian heart than it was in the primal Paradise. Adam never felt in Eden the glow and rapture of the love that fills the heart where much has been forgiven. The pardon of many offences, which deserved death, binds the soul to its merciful Redeemer in stronger ties than creation did or could. He loves much to whom much is forgiven, is a saying of Christ based upon a deep knowledge of the laws of our spiritual being. Look at the woman in the house of Simon the Pharisee. (Luke vii. 36–47.) Deeply wicked had she been, notoriously vicious had been her life. Her " offence was rank, and smelled to heaven." But at length she began to feel a sense of alienation from God, and was pained at the sight of the abyss which her sins had opened between her and the Holy One. She felt the bitter pangs of repentance, and an intense longing for salvation. Convinced of sin, groaning under its crushing weight, and hoping to obtain balm for her wounded heart, she threw herself at the feet of Jesus, moistened them with her tears, wiped them with her hair, and anointed them with the costly ointment. Attracted thus to Jesus for rest to her burdened soul, and deliverance from her uneasy craving for spiritual peace, he lifted from her heart the mountain of despair, pronouncing her sins, which were many, all forgiven, and blotting out, as a thick cloud, her transgressions. When recovered from that moral wreck, how glowing was her love! It was such as Adam felt not in Eden. The greater her sins had been, the more profound had been her desire for redemption, the more she valued the gift of pardon, and the more ardent was her love to the great Restorer. She loved much, for a great debt had been forgiven her. This is a law of our nature. To rescue from a great evil is more highly prized than the bestowal of a great good, without any previous experience of evil. God has bestowed upon us as much as he did upon Adam, and the pardon of sin besides. With us the free gift is of many offences unto justification of life. The pardoned and sanctified sinner is bound to God by the most endearing ties. There can be no doubt that St. Paul loved the Lord with as glowing a love as ever Adam felt in Paradise. Where sin abounded grace did much more abound. That which was evil was overruled for good; yet it was a good which the resources of infinite wisdom might, perhaps, have reached by a different route.

Perfect love has also respect unto degree. All good proceeds from God, who alone is good in himself. His goodness is inherent in his self-existing nature, and is not derived. Created minds are not equally receptive of the divine good, and have not an equal capacity of exercising love. But the law is adapted to the various capacities of created minds. Its language is, "Thou shalt love the Lord thy God with all thy strength," or with all thy power of exercising affection. This is demanded of the child, the peasant, the philosopher, of Adam in Paradise, of every angel before the throne. Each is to love God according to the measure of his capacity. Perfect love is love diffused through our whole being. Every other emotion of the heart is tinged with it, and pervaded by it; it is the warp and woof of every other feeling. The life of such a soul is bound up in the same bundle of life with the Lord its God. Love arrests every fugitive desire, pervades it with itself, and fixes it upon the infinite Good. It erects a chapel in the heart, and there offers ceaseless prayer. The heart desires God above every thing else; in fact there is nothing in earth or heaven it desires besides him, or separate from him; and thus perfect love becomes perpetual prayer. (1 Thess. v. 17.) Prayer is no longer an effort, a task, a labor, but a spontaneity, a life, and as ceaseless as the pulsations of the heart. As rivers flow towards the ocean, as fire ascending seeks the sun, so love rises to its Source, and breathes out itself in unceasing prayer. Love, hidden in the depth of our being, prays even when the mind is occupied with other things. It creates a constant tendency of the spirit towards God, a kind of divine polarity of the soul. The whole life is prayer, one constant flame of devotion. Hence it was the remark of St. Augustine, that "he who loves much prays much, and he who loves little prays little." Christ makes such a heart his constant habitation. The holy flame which perpetually burned in the heart in the original Paradise, and which sin quenched, that divine Promethean spark, Christ has again called down from heaven to animate our lifeless clay. For he came to bring fire on the earth.

Perfect love is the love of God for his own sake as the most perfect Being. We love the Lord because he first loved us. "I love the Lord," says the Psalmist, "because he hath heard my voice and my supplications." (Ps. cxvi. 1.) The consideration of God's goodness and bounty to us in his providence and grace, and especially the great love wherewith he hath loved us in our redemption by the cross, may be, and most commonly is, the spring of our love to him, rather than a consideration of the infinite excellence of his character and nature. But this is only the beginning, and not the perfection, of love. The soul may and ought to love God for his own consummate excellency and moral beauty, independent of all his dealings, and above all the consolations of his grace. May not a parent love a child, or a wife a husband, independent of all their faults or good deeds? The being is abstracted from all his *accidents*, and loved for his own sake. Thus God loves the sinner, while he hates his sins. Thus we are commanded to love our enemies. The man is placed in front of all his evil doings, and his humanity, abstracted from all the evils which do not belong to its essence, is loved. We love the idea of man which that person so imperfectly exhibits. Thus we become followers of God, as dear children, who maketh his sun to rise on the evil and the good, and sendeth rain upon the just and unjust. God loves in the wicked only that which is the work of his own hands, the pure humanity without the unseemly accretions which sin has made to cleave to it. When we thus love our fellow-men, we obey the command, " Be ye perfect, even as your Father in heaven is perfect." (Matt. v. 43–48.) For that precept has reference to the love of our enemies. So the soul may love the pure divinity of God, the simple being of the Deity, abstracted from all his dealings with us. This love of the absolutely perfect One, for his own sake, does not exclude the lower forms of love, but includes them all; just as a whole is made up of all its parts, or a circle of all its segments. We love God, not merely because he is a means to our happiness, which places too slight a value upon him and degrades him, but because he is what he is. The more mature our love is, and the nearer it approaches the love of the celestial world, the less self is regarded, and we seek in God not his gifts, but himself. Abelard well remarks, (A. D. 1108,) " Whoever seeks in God, not himself, but something else, does not

in reality love *him*, but that other thing. . . .
O that we might have so upright a disposition of
heart towards the Lord, as to love him far more
on his own account, because he is so good in
himself, than on account of the benefits which he
brings to us! So would our righteousness render
to him what he claims; that, because he is supremely good, he should be supremely loved by
all. Fear and hope of reward are but the first
step in piety. The fear of the Lord is the *beginning* of wisdom, but the perfection of it is the
pure love of God for his own sake."

There are several forms of fear, which are the
offspring of sin and the root of much of human
misery, which are cast out by perfect love. "There
is no fear in love, but perfect love casteth out
fear." (1 John iv. 18.) Here are two different
mental conditions, which cannot coexist in the
same person. Much of the misery of life is refer-
able to fear. There is no emotion that more disturbs the soul, and is so opposite to that calm
repose and tranquillity which are characteristic of
the purified nature. It is truly said by St. John,
that it hath torment. Did I wish to punish a

person as severely as possible, I would subject him to the dominion of fear; I would keep him in a constant state of alarm and apprehension of some evil. There should be in his heart also a fearful looking-for of judgment and fiery indignation which shall devour the adversaries. Fear exists in many different forms. It assumes Protean shapes. It is sometimes anxiety about the future, a distracting carefulness about the things of to-morrow. Perfect love banishes this from the heart by creating a supreme desire for God. It asks for nothing but the object loved; it wants nothing but the unchanging Good. In the possession of him all the needs of the spirit are met. It casts out the fear of man; that is, a slavish dread of losing the good opinion of our fellow-beings, and an apprehension of personal violence. A consciousness of perfect safety is connected with holy love. It is convinced that nothing can harm us if we are followers of the good One. It puts the soul not only in a position of safety, but of security, which is a freedom from all apprehension of evil. It rests upon the assurance of Christ that all things work together for good to them that love God.

(Rom. viii. 28.) Love, like the magic touch of Midas, changes all objects and events not merely into gold, but into blessings more valuable than gold that perisheth. It is calm in danger. It is the foundation of true courage. It looks peacefully upon the storm of passion and persecution which howls around, like a rainbow over a cataract, watching the madness of the scene. It attaches but a slight value to the applause of the multitude. It is idle wind, empty air. The frowns of the world are nothing, and the soul weeps in secret places at the vanity of popular praise. The favor of God is all. In the perfected heart the fear of death yields to love, though the love of life, which is quite another thing, may still linger. Death is no more a destroying angel, clothed with all the attributes of terror, like the dreadful Samael of the Hebrew popular belief. He is no more a king of terrors, — crushing heart-strings, revelling in groans and pangs, and delighting in blood, like the Odin of the northern mythology, whose name signifies the Mad or Furious One. Love ends this cruel bondage to the fear of death. Death is viewed as the point of eternal union with God, the birth into a higher sphere of life. The fear of the wrath to come is swallowed up by the hope of glory. The perfected soul no more fears death and judgment than did our first parents in a state of innocence. It serves God, not from the dread of his wrath and the fear of hell, which may find place in the heart in a low stage of the divine life, but the love of Christ constraineth. That which is supremely loved cannot be feared, nor its presence dreaded. Hence a servile fear of God, which is the effect of guilt, and which clings to the unsanctified heart, is absorbed by a filial confidence and affectionate familiarity. The idea of the divine presence is painful to the sinner, and the world has been laboring for sixty centuries to banish the Divinity from the universe. He is too near. His eye looks out from the darkness and troubles them, as it did the Egyptians. But the heart where perfect love reigns delights in the divine presence, and feels an ineffable rapture in "being enclosed in his circle, and wrapped up in the lap of his infinite nature." Love removes the thunders from the brow of the Deity, and places there a smile.

All the forms of fear which I have described may exist in different degrees. The scale may be expressed by five terms, each rising above the other; viz., *fear*, *dread*, *terror*, *fright*, and *horror*. But love calms our fear as the harp of David calmed the evil demon in Saul. It is like the whisper of Christ to the storm upon the Sea of Galilee, at the sound of whose creative word the giant billows "sank like sobbing infants to their rest." All the forms of fear, which are the offspring of sin and black night, find no place in the Happy Islands. Instead of the fear that hath torment, there was the calm happiness of unbroken fellowship with God. The souls of the people are imbued with divine love, and pervaded with calmness and peace.

While walking in the blissful groves, and exploring the delightful fields of this island, the soul gained a deliverance from wandering thoughts, especially such thoughts as wander from God, and which arise from evil desires and passions. Love lays siege to the stronghold of the soul, casts down imaginations, and every high thing that exalteth itself against the knowledge of God, and brings into captivity every thought to the obedience of Christ. In the imperfectly sanctified heart, the thoughts break away from the restraints of grace, and roam abroad, whither they please, like a band of lawless banditti. But in the higher position of Christian life, they are taken captive, bound with chains of love, and laid at the feet of Christ. As we naturally think of that we most love, God becomes in the sanctified heart the centre of its thoughts. It requires no struggle to keep the thoughts from straying from the object of supreme love, or to recall them when they have wandered. They are fixed in their orbit by a kind of spiritual gravitation, and spontaneously revolve around their proper centre. As the magnetic needle, when it has been drawn aside from its proper direction, vibrates for a moment back and forth, and then settles down in its natural position, pointing to the polar star, so the mind where perfect love dwells, is sometimes occupied, necessarily, with other thoughts than those of God and heavenly things; but as soon as it is left to itself it becomes fixed upon its divine centre. It requires no effort to think of God, but demands a volition to call off the thoughts from him. The whole current of the soul's life and thought flows in the direction of the supreme Good. The moment the spirit is unoccupied, it finds itself wrapped up in divine contemplation. Even when the hands are employed, the thoughts are with him. Sometimes, in its weakness, the soul almost tires of this contemplation, and says, with the spouse, " Stay me with flagons, comfort me with apples, for I am sick of love." (Cant. ii. 5.) To think of any thing else so much would be unendurable, and the soul would sink under it. But this action is rest. The thoughts have found their appropriate centre, and their proper channel, and there the highest activity is the sweetest repose.

A state which had been apprehended by the mind, and ardently craved, but never realized, I found in the Happy Islands, especially the one I was now exploring, — a state of spontaneous obedience, where duty is not a load, and the law a galling yoke, — where the soul obeys God, just as all material things are subject to their several laws, and as animals and plants obey the instincts of their nature. This is only reached by perfect love. It is the law of our mental nature, that love influences the will so to act as to please the object loved. Genuine love is in the will. It is called *benevolence*, (from *bene*, well, and *volo*, to wish,) or good willing. In this sense it may have God for its object as well as man. Says Christ, "If ye love me ye will keep my commandments;" because perfect love is that position of the will which constitutes the essence of obedience. It contains the living germ of all good actions. The obedience rendered to God by those who dwell in love, is not extorted from unwilling hearts, and chosen as the less of two evils, but it comes of its own accord, without any outward pressure. It is not a chain which the soul reluctantly drags, but a wreath of freedom which it rejoices to wear. We do freely what it is our nature to do. It is as much the nature of perfect love to obey as it is of water to descend an inclined plane. Such an obedience is not work or toil, but rest. The soul again finds its native element, and moves vivaciously and happily in it.

Love is one of the most powerful principles in the universe. Light, which is one of the first of created things, and which may properly be called the shadow of God, exerts a noiseless but potent influence in the vegetable world. With more than an angel's strength, it raises to the surface the millions of vital germs in the seeds buried beneath the soil, and bears upward towards heaven the tall trees of the forest. It paints the face of nature with its infinite variety of coloring, and reveals unnumbered worlds, in the deep abysses of space. Gravity binds every atom and every world to every other atom and world in the universe, so that there is nothing isolated; but all worlds, and systems of worlds, are bound together by its mysterious chain, and move in sublime harmony around their common centre. But love is a greater force in the universe than either. It is the bond of union between all holy intelligences, who are more numerous than the worlds which have been scattered, with such amazing profusion, through the regions of empty space. It is the principle of cohesion in the moral universe, and prevents its crumbling; and conjoins the whole to God. The innumerable company of angels, and the millions of the redeemed, are united by it into one family, with Christ's exalted humanity for its head and centre. It is the principle of unity in the midst of the infinite variety which exists in the spiritual world. Under its influence all contradictions are harmonized, all opposites meet and blend, and all enmities fade away like evening shadows before a rising sun. By its silent and irresistible attraction, it brings into one concordant society or community infants and seraphs, redeemed sinners, and the angels who have kept their first estate, Jews and Gentiles, simple peasants and learned philosophers. The learned and pious Dr. Cudworth, as he felt its rapture in his heart, exclaimed, "O, divine love, the sweet harmony of souls! the music of angels! the joy of God's own heart! the very darling of his bosom! the source of true happiness! the pure quintessence of heaven! that which reconciles the jarring principles of the world! that which melts men's hearts into one another." (Sermon on 1 John ii. 3, 4.) Love is of God, and he who loveth is born of God, and knoweth God. It is a pure emanation of the Divine into finite minds. It comes from God and leads to God. Imagine a region somewhere in the world, some fertile island in the ocean of human depravity, some green *oasis* in the vast Sahara of earth, where love reigns in every heart; just as certainly as things which are equal to the same thing are equal to one another, so he who loves God will love his brother also. Where pure Christian love reigns, Paradise is restored. Such was society in the Happy Islands. God was the centre of affection, where all souls, like the rays of a circle, met and blended in him. Afflictions were encountered by the inhabitants, for they had not yet reached that higher sphere of existence, where sighing grief shall weep no more; but each one felt his brother's sigh, and lightened the load by bearing a part. It is the nature of love to desire to communicate its own happiness to others. In the Happy Islands it is the delight of all to communicate their enjoyments and beatitudes to each other, so that the more there are, the greater is the happiness of the place. They are pervaded with the same divine love, flowing from God, which makes angels ministering spirits to the heirs of salvation. Living on the borders of heaven, the love of heaven fills their souls. Each can say, with the dying Payson, " The nearer I get to heaven, the more I feel of its benevolence, until now I feel an intense desire to wring out to every human being a full cup of blessedness." The spirit of the devoted Backus was here the spirit of all. When informed by his physician that he could not live half an hour, he said, " Then take me from my bed, place me upon my knees, and let me die praying for the world." The very misery in which the world has been involved by sin has given occasion to the highest exhibitions of Christian love. Love has gone out to search among the ruins of our fallen humanity for objects which it may bless. It seeks to bind up the hurts of human nature, and to restore the wreck. It especially yearns over the deep wretchedness of souls destroyed by sin, and sundered from God by the rebellion of their will against his government. It brings the wants of the whole world to the mercy-seat, and makes daily mention of them in prayer. The soul, in its secret aspirations to heaven, addresses the world's Redeemer in language like the following : —

21 *

> "Ah, reign, wherever man is found,
>   My Spouse, belovèd and divine!
> Then am I rich, and then abound,
>   When every human heart is thine.
>
> A thousand sorrows pierce my soul,
>   To think that all are not thine own;
> Ah, be adored from pole to pole; —
>   Where is thy zeal? Arise! Be known."

The love which here reigned went far towards restoring the lost harmony of the outward world. External nature felt its influence. There is a closer connection between the world of mind and the outward world than many suppose. The material creation is the outside circle of created things; it is the rough bark of the universe; the world of mind lies farther inward, towards the vital centre. When love and purity reign in that centre, its influence extends to the circumference, and every thing there feels its power. The flowers bloom with increased lustre, and exhale a sweeter fragrance, when cultivated by the hand of love. It deepens the harmonies of nature. It joins again the sundered links in creation's chain. It binds the human soul to God, and the animal world to man. In the Happy Islands, the enmity of the brute creation had ceased, having been charmed into peace by love. Here was realized the truth, at bottom, in the fable of Orpheus' lyre; of whom it was said, that when he played, the rivers ceased to flow, the rocks, and trees, and animals drew near to listen. Such wonders did love here accomplish. It bound the animal races in its golden chain. There were no more seen ravenous beasts, or venomous reptiles. Every poisonous weed was expelled from the land. No fiery simoom swept its pestilential blast over the fields. Here was no poverty, for the lack of one was supplied by the abundance of others. No selfish heart became the sepulchre of God's blessings, but they were dispensed abroad like a shower of gold. I noticed that life was greatly prolonged in this blessed clime, and diseases were fewer than in any other part of the globe. Many causes contributed to this. A large portion of the diseases which assail us have their origin in the mind. "It is the great art of life to manage well the restless mind." There is a basis of truth in the prayer of Charles Wesley : —

> "Let life immortal seize my clay,
> Let love refine my blood."

Here love had harmonized the passions, controlled the appetites, brought the propensities into their proper sphere of action, and restrained their excesses, and more than all, had banished melancholy. The latter no longer spread a pall of sackcloth over all earthly enjoyments. It gave place to a divine cheerfulness, or what Jeremy Taylor calls "spiritual mirth." Chrysostom describes melancholy as "a cruel torture to the soul, consuming the body and gnawing the very heart." In the Happy Islands, God was the joy of the soul and the health of the countenance. (Ps. xlii. 11.) It is the work of Christ, the great Physician, and the Life of the world, to heal every form of mental disease, and thus to diminish the ailments of the body. The body has no life in itself, but lives from the spirit which has put it on. Hence the mind in its different states is the body's health or malady. We can say, with reference to the evil influence of the passions upon health and longevity, in the language of a writer in the Edinburgh Encyclopedia, "Many fall a sacrifice to anger, grief, or fear; and each of these passions may boast of having killed their tens of thousands. Anger ruffles the mind, hurries on the circulation, and disorders the whole animal and vital functions; and when carried to an extreme, often terminates in fury and madness. Fear and anxiety, by depressing the spirits, not only dispose us to disease, but often render those diseases fatal which an undaunted mind would overcome. Grief is more destructive and more permanent in its effects than either. When indulged, it often changes into a fixed melancholy, which preys upon the system, and wastes the constitution. Experience, indeed, shows that many perish from despondency, who, if they had preserved their vigor of spirits, might have survived many years longer. Neither the irritable, who are agitated by trifles, nor the melancholy, who magnify the evils of life, can expect to attain to a great age. It is the interest, therefore, as well as the duty, of all, who have any regard to their health, to keep these sources of disease and misery under due subjection; and nothing can be more conducive to this, than to regulate our lives by the dictates of religion and virtue. A cheerful temper is the sure attendant of true religion; and cheerfulness is one of the principal characteristics of longevity." When we consider that all these passions are cast out by perfect love, it is not strange that in the Happy Islands there seemed to be a realization of the vision of the prophet, that "there shall be no more thence an infant of days, nor an old man that hath not fulfilled his days; for as the days of a tree are the days of my people, and mine elect shall long enjoy the work of their hands." (Isa. lxv. 20, 22.) Trees, when growing undisturbed, in a favorable soil and climate, live to a great age. They outlive kingdoms. De Candolle found an olive seven hundred years of age, a cedar of Lebanon eight hundred, an oak fifteen hundred, a yew twenty-eight hundred and eighty, a taxodium from four thousand to six thousand years. But the days of God's people were to be like the days of a tree; that is, life should be greatly prolonged. In the Happy Islands, universal cleanliness, and a love of the beautiful, from which it proceeded, had barred the approach of the pestilence; and plenty, which crowned the hills and valleys, set famine at defiance. Here Christianity, which had full sway, had taught the people a reverence for the body as the temple of the Holy Ghost; .had created a sympathy for all forms of suffering; and had caused an advance of all the noble sciences, on which was reared an art of medicine, that went forth to alleviate, if not to heal, all forms of pain and disease. Guided by Christian science, the healing plant came at once to the aid of the sick and weak.

Here I found a place at last where the people never died. Never, until I reached this blissful abode, had I sat down contented under the decree of Providence that men should die, that life should be a mere flash of existence, a spark that should fly upward and expire. Here the yearning of my soul to find a land where death should never come was satisfied. I do not mean that the people of this blissful clime never went out of the world. It is probable that Adam and his posterity would have gone out of the world, had he never sinned. He would have put off these "corporeal impediments," that adapt the spirit to an existence in the natural world, and would have passed into the celestial sphere, where the soul is freed from the material limitations of time and space. But death is not so much the going out of the world, as Jeremy Taylor has truly remarked, as it is the manner of going. To go with fear and trembling, like a slave scourged to a dungeon, — to be forced from light into darkness, and chased out of the world, — that is death. The gospel has *abolished* death, and brought immortal life to light. The inhabitants of these islands realized the truth of our Saviour's declaration at the tomb of Lazarus, that whosoever liveth and believeth in him shall never die. The resurrection, he declared, was ever present with him. " I am the resurrection and the life." The soul, united by faith to its vital source, never comes under the power of death. The curse threatened to Adam is lifted from their condition. Such persons do not *really* die. The body, like the coach which brings the traveller to his home, shall go to the gate of the heavenly mansion, but shall be left without, while the soul alights and enters into rest. So peacefully does the redeemed spirit soar upward to its Source, that it is rather a translation than a dying.

It sinks to rest in the bosom of the infinite Life and Love, as gently as night dews descend upon the flower; nor do weary, worn-out winds expire so soft. The good man languishes into life.

> "Calm as a halcyon, that upon the deep
> Folds slowly its white wings, and fearless falls to sleep."

Death in the Happy Islands was not the king of terrors, but was only a walk at the close of day through a shady vale, along the banks of life's river, accompanied and supported by the good Shepherd. (Ps. xxiii. 4.) In this abode of love, the graveyard was a sleeping place, and Immortality walked among the tombs to guard the peaceful slumberers. Death had lost his sting, and the soul had gained the victory through our Lord Jesus Christ. The cemetery here was " God's-Acre," as the Germans expressively term it, sowed all over amid flowers and fragrant shrubs, that chased away the gloom of death, with precious seed, which shall spring up into a glorious harvest in the great day of redemption. The departure of holy souls from earth is not dying, but transition to immortality. It is an ascent in the scale of being, a going up the celestial ladder into higher degrees of life, of wisdom, and of love. Hence death is used in the New Testament as the symbol of the highest life. "Ye are dead, and your life is hid with Christ in God."

> "There is a world above,
>   Where parting is unknown,
> A whole eternity of love,
>   Formed for the good alone;
> And faith beholds the dying here
> Translated to that happier sphere.
>
> Thus star by star declines,
>   Till all are passed away,
> As morning high and higher shines,
>   To pure and perfect day:
> Nor sink those stars in empty night;
> They hide themselves in heaven's own light."

The land whither I had come to reside was a land of hills and valleys, which drank the rain of heaven, which in "soft silence shed the kindly shower;" a land which the Lord himself cared for, and his eyes were continually upon it from the beginning of the year even unto the end of it. (Deut. ii. 11, 12.) Yet man was placed here to till the ground, as Adam was in Paradise. But having no artificial wants to supply, a few hours of pleasant labor daily were sufficient; and they had ample time for intellectual improvement, for refined social intercourse, and for the worship of God. Wherever two or three met together, either in their dwellings or on the mountain side, or in the valley on the river's bank, they found Jesus in their midst, and realized that it was good to be there. Often did the people exclaim, " Behold, how good and how pleasant it is for brethren to dwell together in unity! It is like the dew of Hermon, and as the dew that descended upon the mountains of Zion ; for there the Lord commanded the blessing, even life forevermore." (Ps. cxxxiii. 1. 2.)

No man locked his dwelling by night; property left by the road side was safe, for love stood sentinel upon the watchtower. No deadly weapon had ever been seen. Peace waved her olive branch over this little world of divine order and harmony. No ardent warriors met " with hateful eyes; " there was no shock of contending armies, like the collision of two icebergs in the ocean. The crow never waded in the blood of the slain, and war never filled the land with the wail of widows and orphans. No neighborhood broils ever occurred. Each one lent to him that asked, hoping to receive nothing again. No one wished to become rich by making others poor. The groan of the bondman was never heard. The hire of the laborer, who had reaped down the field, was not kept back by fraud, nor did his cries for justice against the oppressor enter the ears of the Lord of Sabaoth. Government was pervaded with the spirit of love, and consisted only of a few prudential regulations, which were necessary for the universal good, and with which all cheerfully complied. Christ was really king, and the gospel was the supreme law. Justice returned to earth, and held aloft her even scale. The people went forth in the morning to their daily labor, with songs of praise; and at night, as you passed their dwellings, you heard the voice of prayer. Here were no courts, for love soon settled all differences. Justice was only a form of love. Stern justice, without mercy, is like the light of winter, which wraps the earth in ice. Justice, tempered with love, is like the light of spring, which clothes the earth with flowers. Here were no prisons, for crimes had ceased; no dungeons, whose "echoes only learned to groan." Artificial distinctions faded away before the power of Christian love. There was neither Jew nor Greek, Barbarian, Scythian, bond nor free, male nor female, for all were one in Christ Jesus. Each felt an interest in the welfare of all, and was constrained by Jesus's love to live the servant of all. Love ennobled every service, and every thing was cheerfully done for the good of others, whether to labor to save a world or to kiss away a tear from an infant's eye.

This blissful region, which seemed to occupy a position intermediate between earth and heaven, seemed to be arranged in harmony with the feelings of the sanctified heart. Outward nature is made to image spiritual things. The holy soul looks around upon the glories of creation, and sees in them the symbols of higher things. "They are shadows here, authenticating substance there." How full is the earth of beauty and of blessing! We see eternal love and wisdom reflected every where — the grand and glassy ocean, which, like a boundless mirror, images the deep-blue sky, the glowing sun, the silvery moon, and the ever-

moving panorama of cloud and star, like the ideas
of things existing in the divine mind before they
were embodied in material forms. The material
heavens glowing with countless stars and suns,
which revolve around their common centre, do but
image the numberless societies of the celestial
world, drawn together by spiritual affinities, and
by the nature of that particular form of divine
good in which they are grounded, but all connected with and revolving around Christ, the
universal centre. "The green-carpeted earth, the
infinitely-varied loveliness of the flowers, bedeck-
ing with living gems the land on every side; the
flowering bushes, the fragrant shrubs, the stately
trees, with every shade of foliage, waving their
majestic heads in luxury of life, and ever rising
higher to the light; while over all, the magnificent arch, which constitutes the dome of this
palace of our God, in the still, cerulean hue of
day, and the brilliant blaze of the golden gran-
deur in the night, are full of spiritual significance,
and ever suggest infinitudes of solemn majesty,
order, mercy, and peace." They seem to be ideas
projected from the spiritual world, and assuming,

at this distance from their centre, outward, tangible shapes. This world, so grand, so glorious, seems but the outward robe of the higher spiritual world. It is a heavenly veil, tremulous and wavy, which the Creator has thrown over his inner and more perfect creations. The holy soul, divinely illuminated, may see these spiritual correspondences in the visible world. In the Happy Islands, all outward things were arranged in exact correspondence to their spiritual state. I observed with wonder that all discordant sounds had ceased. Harmonious sounds symbolize divine order in the affections of the soul, and are heavenly in their origin and significance. Discord is infernal, and has its birth in sin. When sin, which is a moral discord in the universe, utters itself freely, the sound is unharmonious. Such is the clangor and discordant roar of the battle field, the yells of a furious mob, the profane oaths and shouts of the wicked in their sensual mirth, and the wailings, and howlings, and gnashing of teeth of the lost. Harmony is from above, and in its spiritual sense represents the state of the soul, when love holds there her peaceful and orderly reign. In the

Happy Islands, all the sweet and varied sounds of nature touched a responsive chord in the redeemed soul, and harmonized with their songs of praise. Nature seemed a vast harp, struck by angel fingers, which expressed and offered up to God the sweet harmony of holy souls. As I walked amid the displays of the divine goodness and wisdom, which every where met my gaze, I could but exclaim, —

> "O for a seraph's golden lyre,
>   With chords of light and tones of fire,
>   To sing Jehovah's love!
> To tell redemption's wondrous plan,
> How God descended down to man,
>   That man might rise above!"

LOVE DUE TO THE CREATOR.

> "And ask ye why He claims our love?
>   O, answer, all ye winds of even,
> O, answer, all ye lights above,
>   That watch in yonder darkening heaven;
> Thou earth, in vernal radiance gay,
>   As when his angels first arrayed thee,
> And thou, O deep-tongued ocean, say
>   Why man should love the Mind that made thee.

There's not a flower that decks the vale,
　There's not a beam that lights the mountain,
There's not a shrub that scents the gale,
　There's not a wind that stirs the fountain,
There's not a hue that paints the rose,
　There's not a leaf around us lying,
But in its use or beauty shows
　True love to us, and love undying."

CHAPTER IX.

THE ISLAND OF ELEUTHERIA.

The Island described. — State of Society. — The Centre of Worship. — The Sabbath. — The Bondage of the Soul ended. — Testimony of heathen Poets and Philosophers to the Tendency of the Soul to Evil. — The Liberty which was enjoyed in Paradise. — Christ restores it to the Soul. — The Soul flows unto God. — The Elements of true spiritual Freedom. — Deliverance from the Bondage to Forms. — Knowledge of the all-satisfying Truth. — The Presence of the Holy Spirit. — Knowledge of the deeper Truths of the Gospel. — Love renders the Soul receptive of Truth. — Three Stages of divine Knowledge. — Divine Wisdom. — The Soul was not only free, but " reigned." — Quotation from Anselm. — A Kingdom of God realized on Earth.

MANKIND HAVE panted for freedom as one of the best blessings which could fall to their lot. Patriots have fought and bled to obtain it for themselves and others. Liberty is dearer to men than life itself. Philosophers and statesmen are eloquent in its praise, and poets, in their divinest strains, sing its surpassing excellence. But few enjoy it, for *true* freedom is not merely an external condition, but an inward state. "He whom the Son maketh free is free indeed." (John viii. 36.) In the Happy Islands men were both outwardly and inwardly free.

The Island of Eleutheria was not like the others of the group, divided into private farms and gardens, but was the common property of all. In extent it was nearly equal to the others. It contained a beautiful lake, dotted with fertile islets. The public gardens were on one of them, containing all the rare plants and productions of the world, and constituting a miniature Paradise. Here were parks, and fountains, and public walks, and baths. The public buildings of this peaceful commonwealth were situated on the Island of Eleutheria. On one of the islets of the lake stood the edifice containing the public library. In this quiet and delightful retreat one could not avoid a desire to retire and hold converse, by means of books, with the wisest and holiest men of past ages and all lands. In places surrounded with unsurpassed beauty stood the schools and seminaries for the

Christian education of the young. Here science and art were the constant companions of virtue and religion. Every thing which could stimulate the natural depravities of the heart was banished, for it was not a race of angels that was to be educated, but the offspring of sinful Adam. Every thing which could raise the mind from the natural plane of life to a spiritual existence was employed. Nothing is more potent to accomplish this than divine truth. Hence spiritual truths were deposited in the tender mind of childhood, which became the germs of a spiritual life. The children, at an age when they were peculiarly susceptible of permanent impressions, when their character was in its formative stage, were brought under the combined influence of pious parental discipline and example, of a truly Christian education, in the public schools and seminaries, and of the redeeming power of the church and ministry. The Holy Spirit, which is never absent from his truth, came like genial sunshine and rain upon the seed sown. The growth of evil in the heart was checked and stunted; every good principle was educed; and the soul, born under the dominion of the earthy and sensuous, was raised to that which is spiritual and heavenly. The schools were free for all, and the scholar, without private expense, passed through the several gradations up to the university, where he enjoyed the highest collegiate and professional instruction. All the mechanical trades were taught on scientific principles. The noble science of agriculture, the employment of man in the original Paradise, was taught to all the youth. The effect was seen in the astonishing fertility and beauty of the lands. The country spread out before you like a celestial landscape. It was relieved in a great measure from the primal curse, and became, like the valley of the Nile, or the Garden of the Lord. Sometimes I ascended a hill which overlooked the islands. A more enchanting prospect the eye never beheld, than was opened before me. I looked down upon peaceful villages, vine-clad cottages, and splendid mansions encompassed with gardens, stately trees, flower beds, and fields. When seen glittering in the sun, the leaves of the trees seemed to be formed of silver, and the fruit of gold. Here was the abode of domestic peace and contentment, which made each family a heaven on a diminished scale. Every thing was radiant with peace and transporting joys. Flocks and herds wandered over the hills and plains, and water fowls gambolled in the lakes. There were a great number of fruit trees, and forests of lofty growth, and meandering streams, and waving fields of grain, "a sea of verdure rioting in the wealth of its ripening harvests." In spring, the air was embalmed by a vast profusion of flowers blossoming on the lemon, orange, and a thousand sweet-scented shrubs, and was as pure and balmy as Eden itself.

In the Island of Eleutheria was the national cathedral, a Christian temple, where at stated times the whole population met for the worship of God. It stood on an eminence overlooking the adjacent gardens and fields. It was a beautiful and imposing structure, where all classes mingled to adore the common Father. It was sufficiently large to accommodate many thousands. Here all ages and sexes met to worship God in spirit and in truth. Sometimes the multitude assembled in an adjoining park, which had been fitted up for the purpose. This was the case the first Sabbath which I spent in the Happy Islands. The day is fragrant with sacred memories, and can never be forgotten while life lingers. All nature seemed to repose and put itself in correspondence to the day and the occasion. A deep, calm, and holy feeling pervaded my whole being. It seemed as if my spirit was reposing with God on the first Sabbath after creation : —

> ' How still the morning of the hallowed day!
> Mute is the voice of rural labor, hushed
> The ploughboy's whistle and the milkmaid's song;
> The scythe lies glittering in the dewy wreath
> Of tedded grass, mingled with fading flowers,
> That yestermorn bloomed waving in the breeze;
> The faintest sounds attract the ear—the hum
> Of early bee, the trickling of the dew,
> The distant bleating midway up the hill.
> Calmness seems throned on yon unmoving cloud.
> To him who wanders o'er the upland leas,
> The blackbird's note comes mellower from the dale,
> And sweeter from the sky the gladsome lark
> Warbles his heaven-tuned song; the lulling brook
> Murmurs more gently down the deep-sunk glen;
> While from yon lowly roof, whose curling smoke
> O'ermounts the mist, is heard, at intervals,
> The voice of psalms, the simple song of praise."

At length, during this Sabbatic rest of nature, the soft music of the church bell rolled over the echoing hills and through the quiet vales, summoning, as with angel tones, the multitudes to the place of prayer, the house of God. From every direction, the people were seen wending their way from all the islands to this attractive centre, the place where the Lord had recorded his name, and where he had promised ever to meet his children and bless them. The aged and the young, parents and children, and neighbors, in groups, clad with neatness, approach the holy place, until all are seated in the grove, behind the public temple. Each breathes a silent prayer for the divine benediction, and holds his soul for a few moments in the presence of God, solemnly worshipping him, and fixing every desire upon him as the fountain of blessing. A placid stillness reigns; calmness pervades every heart, and is enstamped on every countenance. The man of God, the servant of the Lord Jesus Christ, venerable for his years and holy wisdom, reads the word of God; the multitude, as with one heart and voice, fill the dome of heaven with a song of praise. It was like the sound of many waters, and seemed to place us in living sympathy with the angelic choirs. Then, as if prostrated by some invisible power, the whole multitude fell upon their knees, and bowed before "the name high over all." The very act was a sublime prayer, and seemed typical of the holier worship of the heavens, —

> "Where ranks of shining thrones around
> Fall worshipping, and spread the ground."

The voice of supplication from the pulpit, in silver tones, rolled over the prostrate throng. Prayer ardent opened heaven; both worlds flowed together. "The Lord is in this place," was the secret feeling of every heart. The scene was one surpassing description. The discourse of the man of God; the simple and united songs of praise which melted all hearts into one; the absence of all pomp and formality, and yet the reign of divine order; the cheerful solemnity which overshadowed the place; the intermingling of instruction and devotion, so that the wants of the intellect and heart were both met; the absence of Pharisaic legalism, and the presence of Christian freedom, which took its place, and made the Sabbath a delight of the Lord, holy and honorable; all this

made the scene morally sublime, and the occasion
rich in the experience of divine things. Christ
has said, " Where any two shall agree [or har-
monize — for the word is borrowed from music] as
touching any thing they shall ask, it shall be
done." But here thousands of hearts, like so
many musical strings in tune, blended their desires
into one vast symphony, which rose to the throne
of God.

The Sabbath, in the Happy Islands, was a day
of holy convocation, as it would have been in
Paradise, had sin never expelled the race. It
served to unite the soul to the Lord, and by the
communion of saints on earth and in heaven, to
join heart to heart, and conjoin this lower sphere
of life to the celestial realms. By bowing together
before the same Creator and Redeemer, and fixing
the soul upon the same divine and universal centre, all aristocratic distinctions vanished, public
spirit was kept alive, unity was maintained in the
midst of diversity, and a family feeling pervaded
the whole commonwealth. Heart met heart in
holy love. Every expression of good will for the
welfare of others was echoed back from a congenial

spirit. This was to me my first *real* Sabbath. It was never enjoyed before in all the fulness and extent of its spiritual significance. The Sabbath, in its lowest natural sense, is a day of cessation from bodily labor, after six days of physical toil. In a higher sense, it is a divine symbol of the peace that attends regeneration, when the soul becomes tranquil, no longer agitated by fear, by anxiety, or conscious guilt, or any evil passions, which create an inward disturbance. This has been expressively called "the rest of faith," "the Sabbath of divine love." In a still higher sense, the Sabbath is a type of that profound and unutterable repose and quietism of a soul that has returned from all its wanderings to an eternal union with the Lord. It is a type of that endless Sabbatism that remains for the people of God. A Sabbath enjoyed in the fulness of its meaning leaves the sweet savor of its influence upon the spirit during the whole week, and makes life a perpetual rest. After the public services of the day had ended, and the sun had gone down in glory, I retired to spend the night upon an islet of the lake. The silent moon, in her majestic beauty, glided slowly through a cloudless sky, deluging the whole land with the soft radiance of her tranquil light. The same stars that shone upon Eden, and that once looked down upon the Son of God, and listened to the fervor of his prayers, while he knelt in the solitude of the mountain at the midnight hour, glittered still with undiminished splendor. It was a night of holy meditations and communings. The soul floated on the ocean of the divine presence. All things whispered of God. Nature, in divine melody, proclaimed her Maker: —

"From mountain and forest an organ-like tone,
From hill-top and valley a mellower one;
Stream, fountain, and fall, whispered low to the sod,
For the word that they spoke was the name of our God.

All night, as if stars were deserting their posts,
The heavens were bright with the swift-coming hosts!
While the sentinel mountains, in garments of green,
With glory-decked foreheads were seen."

In the Happy Islands, the soul was restored to its native freedom. In the country I had left, my spirit had been in a state of bondage, — a most galling servitude. This moral condition is most forcibly described by St. Paul, in the seventh chapter of the Epistle to the Romans. He personates that state, because he had passed through it; it had once been his own experience. The strength of the depraved tendency becomes fully realized in our consciousness only when we set ourselves in opposition to it, just as the force of a river's current is only perceived when we attempt to row against it. When Paul first attempted to break the fetters of sin, he clearly apprehended their strength. He found a law in his members that, when he would do good, evil was present with him. This tendency of his nature to evil was as invariable as the law of gravitation in matter, or of instinct in animals. His mind, his reason, and his conscience were illuminated to see what was right and good, but his heart was not renewed so as to enable him to act in harmony with his sense of obligation. There was an inward schism in his nature; the soul was at war with itself. He was conscious of what was right, and yet did what he knew to be wrong. He formed purposes of obedience, — for to will was present with him, — but failed to execute his resolutions. The good that he would he did not. He travelled hard, but made no advance, like a criminal on a tread-mill, or a horse turning a shaft in a circle. But he found deliverance through Christ. At the sight of the cross his fetters fell. In self-despair he cried, " O, wretched man that I am! who shall deliver me from the body of this death?" He discovered in Christ the freedom the soul had lost by the original transgression. The law of the Spirit of life in Christ Jesus made him free from the law of sin and death. This freedom was not merely an outward obedience, like the artificial and spasmodic motions of a dead body under the influence of galvanism; but it was a living impulse within, originating in a restoration of his infected and enfeebled nature. It was not the performance of the outward duties of religion, coldly acted over as a task, just as an animal may be trained to perform things above its nature, but an interior soul and principle of divine life. The old man, with his corrupt tendencies, was put off; and the soul, renewed in its inmost centre, put on the new man; which, after God, is created in righteousness and true holiness. (Eph. iv. 22–24.) His soul became a receptacle of the life of Christ, and it was then his *nature* to live Christ-like. The law of the Spirit of life in Christ Jesus pervaded his inmost being, and he lived because Christ lived, just as the branch lives and bears fruit by virtue of its conjunction with the parent trunk. The good acts of the soul are not then like the external adornments of a Christmas tree, which have no vital connection with the tree, but are, like the natural fruit, the living outgrowth of the branches. There can be no real freedom while the corrupt nature remains unchanged. We may labor to filter the streams, but the corrupt fountain still pours forth its bitter waters.

The heathen philosophers and poets have not failed to observe the tendency of human nature to evil. Juvenal, in harmony with the teachings of Paul concerning the carnal mind, (Rom. vii. 18–23.) declares, that *Nature, unchangeably fixed, runs back to wickedness, as bodies to their centre.* Aristotle calls this struggle of the enslaved moral powers against the domination of the fleshly and selfish propensities *the natural repugnance of man's temper to reason.* Pythagoras terms it *the fatal companion, the noxious strife, that lurks within us, and which was born with us.* Cicero laments that man is brought into the world by nature, with a frail and infirm body, *and a soul prone to divers lusts.* This inward contradiction, this struggle of the enslaved spirit against the deep current of the depraved propensities, led Seneca, one of the purest of pagan moralists, to say, "What is this, Lucilius, which draws us in another direction from that in which we endeavor to go, and impels us whither we desire to retreat? What is it which wrestles as it were with our souls, and will not permit us even once to do what we wish?" Plato was led to set forth the soul, under the image of a chariot, which two horses were drawing, the one white, and the other black. Thus the depravity of human nature is a truth of universal consciousness.

In man's original state the lower animal or earthly propensities were in perfect subjection to his higher moral nature, which connects us with the Deity, and they were spiritual in their action. In our fallen state, this inward harmony is lost; the balance of our powers is disturbed. That which was made to rule is held in vassalage. It is what Solomon in symbolical language describes as the vanity of our earthly condition. "I have seen servants upon horses, and princes walking as servants upon the earth." (Eccl. x. 7.) This subserviency of the spirit to the flesh, which is the condition we have inherited from Adam, is what Dr. Chalmers denominates "the great unhingement" of the soul. Christ came to restore the disturbed relations of the powers of the soul. He does not annihilate any thing which belongs to the essence of human nature, but reinstates the dethroned moral and spiritual faculties, which constitute the point of attachment between us and God, just as the lower propensities link us to the animal world, and when predominant disjoin the soul from God, its proper centre. Thus by the redeeming scheme of Christianity is accomplished the removal of the disunion between the created spirit and the Divinity; the soul is brought into divine order; its bent of sinning is removed; the direction of its nature's current is changed. Before, its affections tended to the earth; now, to the heavens. Sin cleaved to it, and the struggling and inthralled spirit could not cast off the works of darkness;

now, it experiences a great facility in the performance of holy actions.   In Paradise the law was
written upon man's heart; that is, its demands
were in perfect harmony with his affections.   It
was a law of liberty, because we do with delight
and with freedom what we love to do.   Liberty is
the offspring of love, and the character of a man's
freedom is according to the nature of his ruling
love, in which he is grounded.   In man's primitive
condition the law was so incorporated into his
spiritual being, that he did the things contained
in the law from the tendency of his nature.   The
restoration of this state is included in the terms
of the new and better covenant of Christianity.
Christ came not merely to write, "Holiness to the
Lord," upon Aaron's forehead, or upon the breast-
plate of the high priest; but, "This is the covenant
which I will make with the house of Israel after
those days, saith the Lord.   I will put my laws
into their minds, and will write them upon their
hearts." (Heb. viii. 10.)   The intellect shall be
so illuminated as to see what is right and duty,
and the affections so purified as to embrace them
cheerfully and freely.   This inward law of liberty

and life is the law of love. This does not release
the soul from any moral obligation, but renders
obedience the natural working of the spirit. The
soul is a law unto itself. In a qualified sense it
is a freedom from all law without us, a deliverance from the Pharisaic bondage to the letter, and
the living spirit of the law pervades and assimi-
lates to itself the whole interior nature. If the
soul where love reigns supreme could be taken
out of the domain of the external commandment,
and be left to do as it pleased, it would do the
things contained in the law, just as a body left to
itself tends towards the centre of the earth. Hence
said St. Augustine, "*Habe caritatem, et fac quic-
quid vis*" — Have charity, and do what you please.
Thus it is a state of the purest liberty, for the
soul, impelled by love, does what it chooses; and
it is also a state of the sweetest bondage. The
soul is united to the Divinity, like a plant to its
primary, and from an inward impulse revolves
around its blissful centre. This subjection through
love is sweeter than to possess empires. It is a
state of the *largest* liberty. A criminal may be
free within the contracted dimensions of his cell.

In that limited area he may be a monarch. He may even dream of roaming at large over the hills and fields, but wakes to find his limbs locked in iron fetters, and his person confined within the limits of a dungeon. The gospel sets our feet in a large place. In an omnipresent Deity the soul finds an element where it has infinite room. Within the boundless circle of the divine nature, and limitless sphere of the divine presence, it moves and lives.

In the second chapter of Isaiah, the prophet, in speaking of the age of the Messiah, says, "It shall come to pass in the last days, that the mountain of the Lord's house shall be established in the top of the mountains, and shall be exalted above the hills; and all nations shall flow unto it." (Isa. ii. 2.) We can never deem the work of our redemption complete until we do good without effort, just as the sinner does evil. As the torrents of the mountains, as the rivers in the valleys, flow to the ocean from the law of their own nature, so the soul fully regenerated *flows* towards the mountain of God's holiness from its own inward impulse. It is not impelled merely by a sense of obligation, but through the attractions of love, it silently, calmly, and freely moves in the line of duty. The degree of ease with which one does what is right, is the measure of the degree of our redemption. In the highest stage of our personal regeneration, our whole inward nature is transformed into the image of the heavenly, and the current of life flows spontaneously in the direction of God and holiness. The thoughts, the affections, the desires, and even the will, all tend of their own accord towards their natural centre. Such a soul does right without a struggle with opposing tendencies, without an effort, and sometimes without knowing it. It is not driven by conscience to duty, (for instance, to communion with God by secret prayer,) like a slave to a task. Its nature *flows* in that direction. Such a person acts in accordance with the law, and yet is not pressed by the law, or the demands of conscience, but his nature, his life, is to do what the law demands. His soul has recovered its native freedom, the freedom of angels and of God. This is to be, according to Isaiah, the uniform experience of the redeemed in the progress of Christ's redemptive work. The time will come when the multitudes of the world will *flow* unto the mountain of the Lord's house, not like the Euphrates, in a great, rapid, and impetuous current, roaring and dashing, but the ransomed spirit shall flow to God like the gentle Siloah, whose waters go softly. (Isa. viii. 6, 7.) "All the rivers run into the sea, yet the sea is not full; to the place whence the rivers come, thither they return again." (Eccl. i. 7.)

One element of the liberty enjoyed in the Happy Islands was a deliverance from the bondage to outward forms. When removed from the worn channel of external rites, in which its life had once flowed, the soul still lived. The truth of the remark of Archbishop Fenelon was realized, that "those who have experienced the grace of sancti- fication in its higher degrees have not as much need of set times and places for worship as others. Such is the purity and strength of their love, that it is very easy for them to unite with God in acts of inward worship at all times and in all places. They have an interior closet. The soul is their temple, and God dwells in it." They every where find Him who declared himself greater than the temple. They are in a limited degree in the state described by St. John as belonging to the New Jerusalem, where there was no temple, for the Lord God Almighty and the Lamb are the temple of it. (Rev. xxi. 22.) Through the new principle of divine life which they have received, they are able to render a true spiritual worship every where. Their whole life is a perpetual sacrifice of praise and prayer. One reason why they do not need fixed times and places of worship so much as persons in the first stage of Christian life is, because they are not moved so much, in their heavenward way, by influences lying out of themselves, as are beginners in religious experience. They are impelled by a principle of life deep seated within. They are not compelled, like the heaven-storming Titans of the Greek mythology, in rising to the celestial regions, to pile mountains upon the top of mountains, but their regenerated spirits, restored to their original harmony with themselves and with heaven, and freighted with the very element of the glorified state, rise of their own accord and join the worship above. They do not, like the Titans, mount into the heavens by any external and material means of communication, but by Christ, who is always present to them, and communion with whom is heaven. Their liberty has not made them free from worship, but "emancipated them into the captivity of worship." Such persons are more punctual in their attendance upon the ordinary means of grace, such as public, social, and private devotion, than others in a lower degree of divine life. These means of grace are like the beautiful gate of the temple, where the beggar stationed himself every day to receive alms; not because he hoped for a blessing from the place, but from those who passed through it. When providentially deprived of the means of grace, they can live without them. Yet both for their own good and the profit of others, they are found in their places in the public congregation, and the more social seasons of prayer and praise.

In this delightful abode of peace and love, a people were found who were truly free. They had perfect freedom in their outward, social, and civil condition. All obstacles to the pursuit of happiness and right action were removed. The truth had made them free. Without the word of God, possessed and appropriated so as to leaven the life of the people, no community has ever enjoyed freedom, whatever may have been the form of their government. The boasted liberty of Greece and Rome, so much sung by poets, and admired by statesmen and philosophers, was not real freedom. "He is the freeman whom the truth makes free." In this peaceful Christian republic, the word of God was not only in every house, but in every heart; so that no one could say to his neighbor, "Know the Lord, for all knew him from the least to the greatest." Hence they enjoyed the glorious liberty of the sons of God. (Rom. viii. 21.) Christ came to proclaim liberty to the captive spirit, and the opening of the prison to souls that were bound in sin and nature's night. The year of jubilee, when liberty was proclaimed throughout the land of Israel unto all its inhabitants, and when every man was restored to the heritage of his fathers, was a shadow of good things to come in the Messianic age. Said Christ, "Ye shall know the truth, and the truth shall make you free." But what is the all-satisfying truth which brings liberty to the enslaved spirit, and where is it to be found? It is the knowledge of what constitutes the supreme good; not a mere intellectual apprehension, but an experimental knowledge of it. He can never be free who seeks his highest good in the creatures, and not in the Creator; who seeks for rest in any thing that is not God. One of the greatest falsities in the universe is an expectation that created things, however excellent, can satisfy the infinite longings of the human spirit. The day of freedom has dawned upon that soul which has learned at the feet of Christ, that things seen and temporal are insufficient for its bliss; and which has taken the Deity in all his infinite attributes as its portion — his omnipresence as the extent of its inheritance, and his eternity as the period of its enjoyment. The free spirit is no longer enslaved to the creatures, no longer loaded down with thick clay. The slavery of inordinate and unsatisfied desire is terminated. Who is so free as that man, whose soul has found in its own depth the supreme good, and desires nothing except what it now possesses? In God it has all. Out of God, and sundered from him, the whole material universe is worthless. The constant tendency of such a soul is towards God. His freed affections and desires rise from the things of earth, where they had been entwined and entangled, and fix peacefully upon the centre of their rest. The law of sin is reversed, and becomes an inward law of liberty. The Psalmist prays for this, and all the more earnestly, as he had become entangled in the yoke of bondage. "Create in me a clean heart, O God; and renew a right spirit within me. Restore unto me the joys of thy salvation; and uphold me by thy free Spirit." (Ps. li. 10–12.)

The presence of the Spirit of God in the soul is necessary to its liberty. To be filled with the Spirit, to be baptized with the Holy Ghost, and to walk in the Spirit, is to be restored to the original divine fellowship enjoyed in the primitive Paradise, and lost by sin. The Holy Spirit is the every where present medium of communication between the human heart and the Father and the Son. It is by the Spirit that the Divinity imparts himself to men. The soul is free only so far as its selfhood dies and it is pervaded with the life of God. When it is brought within the sphere of the divine efflu- ence, and the divine life flows into it, so that it can say, "It is no longer I that liveth, but Christ liveth in me," then it has found its native freedom. It is only where the Spirit of the Lord is that there is true liberty. When he is in the heart, and operates without obstruction, we behold with unveiled face the glory of the Lord, and are changed into the same image from glory to glory, as by the Spirit of the Lord. The Holy Spirit is called by David a free Spirit, not merely because he is freely bestowed upon the world, but because he sets the soul at liberty from sin by creating in it all holy dispositions and tempers, takes away the spirit of bondage to fear, supplies its place with the spirit of adoption, and enables us to serve and worship God, not as slaves, but as sons. By imparting to us the divine nature, we share the bliss and partake of the freedom of God.

The Spirit makes the soul free by leading it into the essential, imperishable, and all-satisfying truth. Under its tuition the soul advances from the first rudimentary principles into the deep things of God. He is the Spirit of truth, and he in whose heart he ever dwells has in himself the very fountain and substance of truth. The Holy Spirit takes the place of Christ's material presence. The divine Paraclete is the great Teacher. It was profitable for the disciples that Jesus, as to his material manifestation, left the world. It was necessary in order to remove from their minds their sensuous notions of the kingdom of God. He had many things to say to them concerning his doctrine, but they were not in a condition to bear them. Their souls were not receptive of the higher truths of the gospel. "It was the pleasure of the holy Trinity," says Euthymius, "that the Father should *draw* them to the Son, that the Son should *teach* them, and the Holy Spirit should *perfect* them. The two first things were already completed; but it was necessary for the third to be accomplished, namely, the being perfected by the Holy Spirit." To be perfect, in the New Testament sense, is to be fully initiated into the mysteries of the gospel, into the deeper truths of the kingdom of God. It is to rise from the lowest elementary principles to a maturity and fulness of Christian knowledge, and to enjoy a corresponding inward experience. (Heb. vi. 1.) It is to reach the maturity of Christian manhood. "When that which is perfect is come, then that which is in part is done away. When I was a child I spake as a child, I thought as a child, I understood as a child; but when I became a man I put away childish things." (1 Cor. xiii. 10, 11.) This can only be reached under the powerful tuition of the Paraclete, or Comforter, who is to be in us and to abide with us forever. Love, which is one of the first fruits of the Spirit, furnishes the soul that disposition which is most receptive of divine truth. It has an affinity for truth. It drinks in the truths of the kingdom of God, as a dry soil drinks in the rain of heaven. Such a soul instinctively knows of the doctrine of Christ, and discerns truth from error. Pure love is the essence of all divine truth. Hence Christ declares that to love God with all the heart, and the neighbor as ourselves, is the whole law and the prophets. Where pure love exists, truth flows in, just as light penetrates and illuminates a transparent medium. The earth without an atmosphere to receive and retain the light of the heavens would be enveloped in darkness, though innumerable suns might be flaming in the firmament. So love is the atmosphere of the human spirit, which receives and holds the spiritual truths of the divine word. Without it the understanding is darkened.

It has seemed to some that the work of redemption has passed through three successive stages or dispensations, corresponding to the three persons in the Trinity. The times of the Old Testament belong to God the Father; in this period he reveals himself in his self-existence, his unity, and almighty power, by signs and wonders. Next followed the times of the New Testament, in which the incarnate Word revealed himself in his wisdom, where the strivings after a comprehensible knowledge of spiritual mysteries predominates. The seeds of knowledge and the germs of spiritual ideas were deposited by Christ in the soil of the human mind, to be unfolded in the future history of the church. In this epoch of redemption light struggles with the thick darkness, and celestial and spiritual truth strives for admission and habitation in the fleshly mind. We are now in the dispensation of the Holy Spirit, which commenced on the day of Pentecost. In this the fire of divine love predominates. The germs of thought sown by

Christ in the consciousness are stimulated and vivified by the presence of the Spirit, and a mature and glorious harvest of wisdom is the result.

The *individual* also passes through three successive stages of divine knowledge; for the individual differs from the church as a whole only as a small circle differs from a large one. Both are subject to the same laws of development and progress. The infantile and sensuous ideas of God and heavenly things give place, in the progress of our salvation, to a higher and more spiritual knowledge of God and the things of God. Lastly, the soul, in the fellowship of the Holy Spirit, attains to rest and freedom in the possession of celestial wisdom. The mind in its restless craving for knowledge can never be free and enjoy tranquillity until it attains the unspeakable gift of the wisdom that comes from above. Once it restlessly searched for knowledge as for a hidden treasure; now it seeks for wisdom. Wisdom is the soul, the inmost essence of knowledge. It is the holy of holies of knowledge, which the soul enters by passing inward through the outward court of sense, and the sanctuary of mere religious science.

Knowledge without it is empty wind; it is worldly in its origin, and can never elevate the soul above the world. The soul at first is in the lowest story, the basement of the palace of truth, a mere sensuous apprehension of things. It then rises to the next higher stage, the second story, which is what we call religious knowledge. It is the science of the Christian schools. It is the dawn of spiritual light. It is like a luminous cloud which has concealed the sun in its bosom. By wisdom, the soul is elevated to the upper story of the palace, and moves in the angelic plane of intellectual life. How vast the difference between the meek wisdom of a divinely illuminated mind and that mere secular knowledge which is wholly disconnected from God, and falsely called science. Unless knowledge leads the soul to God, it is worthless and unsatisfying. True wisdom comes down from God and leads to him. It is not a native of earth, but of heaven, and draws the soul to the seat of its rest. It does not enter the soul through the senses, but is a high and divinely bestowed intelligence, imparted to a soul in union with the Deity. It includes in it holiness, divine

25 *

freedom, and peace. It contains in it, as a gem in a casket, the chief good, " for which every man, by virtue of the deepest and inmost want of his nature, cannot but long." It was the companion of God, in the solitude of his own eternity, before he created the world. It filled the divine mind with infinite happiness; and its possession by the finite mind cannot but impart the purest bliss. (Prov. viii. 22–29.) The soul must soar above the world to find the fountain of this heavenly wisdom. It is a hidden wisdom which none of the princes of this world know. It is the wisdom of God in a mystery, which we speak among them that are perfect, and which God ordained for our glorification, before the foundation of the world. (1 Cor. ii. 7.) It is obtained only by direct communication of the soul with God, through the Holy Spirit. As the divine presence moves over the abyss of the human spirit, it gives vitality to the germs of wisdom, hidden there by Christian instruction, and they become fruitful. What a weight of meaning do the Scriptures then contain! A verse becomes a volume. We find that all our previous inquiries have only ruffled the surface;

and we see their meaning reaching down into the unfathomed depth of infinity. Before the soul is bathed in that celestial light in which God dwells, and before it is baptized with the Holy Spirit, in reading the divine word, "the light shineth in the darkness, and the darkness comprehendeth it not." Before the mind receives the unction from the Holy One, who is truth itself, and who teaches us all things, the mind is enslaved to the outward letter, and to sense, as were the apostles themselves before they received the Pentecostal influences. The baptism of the Spirit elevates the soul from merely natural knowledge to a higher plane of spiritual intelligence.

In the Happy Islands, the people were not only free, in the fullest sense of that term, but they reigned. Here was found a royal priesthood. They were all kings and priests unto God. I never comprehended the hidden meaning of this until I gained this pleasant land, where Christianity exerted its full influence in shaping the inner and outward life of the inhabitants. In the heaven to which we hasten there is but one will; that is, all individual wills, without losing their personality, are merged and lost in the will of God. To reign with Jesus, to sit with him on his throne, and to be exalted to the kingly dignity and position, is not to govern, under him, any particular province of his unbounded empire, but to have one will with him. Then, whatever the soul wills or desires, it *has ;* because its will and desires are in harmony with God's will. To have what we will is absolute monarchy, which never really exists in the kingdoms of the world, but only in the sanctified heart. For what earthly monarch ever had his will in all things? The purified heart more truly reigns than does the Czar of Russia, or the Sultan of Turkey. For it has exactly what it desires, because it wants nothing in earth or heaven contrary to the will of God, and every thing which he wills comes to pass. This state characterizes the highest form of the Christian experience in this world, but will be more complete in the celestial state. The pious Anselm (born in Aosta, in Piedmont, in A. D. 1033 — died 1109) clearly apprehended the blessedness of that most intimate of all unions, the conjunction of the human and the divine will,

which is the prime element of the heavenly state.
He says, "My dear brother, God calls and asks
you to bid for the kingdom of heaven. This
kingdom of heaven is one whose blessedness and
glory no mortal eye hath seen, no ear hath heard,
and no heart of man can conceive. But that thou
mayst gain some idea of it, take the following
illustration: Whatever any one, who is thought
worthy of reigning there, *wills*, that, whether in
heaven or on earth, *is done*. For so great will be
the love between God and those who are to be in
this kingdom, and of the latter, one towards the
other, — that all will love each other as they do
themselves, and God more than they do themselves.
Hence no one there will be disposed to will any
thing else except what God wills, and what one
wills all shall will, and what one or all may will,
God shall will. It will therefore be with every
individual and with all, with the whole creation,
and with God himself, as each shall will. And thus
shall all be perfect kings, for that *shall be* which
each *wills ;* and all will be at the same time with
God as one king, — as it were one man, — because
all shall will the same thing, and what they will,

shall be. God from heaven asks you to bid for such a good. Does any inquire, For what price? He is answered, He who will give the kingdom of heaven, demands no earthly price; and to God, to whom belongs every thing which exists, no one can give what he had not. And yet God does not give so great a good for nothing; for he gives it to none who do not love it; for no one gives that which he dearly values to him who cares nothing about it. Therefore *love* and *possess*. Finally, since to reign in heaven is nothing else than to be so united by love into one will with God, all holy angels and men, as that all at the same time possess the same power, love God more than thyself, and thou beginnest already to possess what thou wilt have there in a perfect manner. But this love cannot be a perfect one in thee, unless thou makest thy heart free from all other love; for like a vase which, the more you fill it with water or with any other fluid, will hold so much the less oil, so the heart excludes *this* love in the same proportion as it is carried away with some other love." (Neander's History of Christianity and the Church, vol. iv. p. 366.) Love is the principle of union; it is spiritual conjunction. It sustains the same relation to the spiritual world that gravity does to the material. Love makes many into one; selfishness is the opposite. It destroys unity; it disperses abroad. It renders impossible the conjunction of many into one whole.

The above ideal of the kingdom of God was more fully realized in the Happy Islands than in any other place which I had ever seen. In this peaceful commonwealth, pervaded as it was by Christianity, as the Roman empire once was by idolatry, was the realization in actual life of a kingdom of God on earth. The Christian spirit interpenetrated the whole fabric of society, and here was seen what St. Augustine calls a *Civitas Dei*, a State of God, a City where God reigns. It was a New Jerusalem, an incipient millennium. Here was the dawning of the latter-day glory. The golden age came back to earth, and Paradise was restored. It seemed an Aurora heralding a celestial day. "Behold, the tabernacle of God is with men, and he will dwell with them, and they shall be his people, and God himself shall be with them, and be their God." In this place, where the redeemed soul walked with a present Deity, there was a complete abstraction from ten thousand things, which, in the noisy world, create discord and disturbance in the minds of men. Peace was not a transient gleam amid the general gloom, but a fixed mental condition. It was not a rainbow, arching the roaring, foaming waters of the cataract, but like what the traveller sees in the north of Europe — a sun that sinks not beneath the horizon, but gilds the mountain tops with his beams at midnight, and enfolds the earth with his almost celestial glory.

CHAPTER X.

THE ISLAND HENOTIA, OR THE STATE OF DIVINE UNION.

Numa searching for God. — The Deity every where. — He is to be sought within. — Augustine. — The primitive Philosophies. — The Hindu Philosophy. — Its Aim. — Fundamental Error. — The Conjunction of the Humanity of Jesus with the Father. — Annihilation of our Selfhood. — Charles Wesley. — Madame Guyon. — The Allness of God. — Losing ourselves in him. — Kempis. — Union with the Deity Man's primitive Condition. — Christ the Way. — The hypostatical Union. — How Conjunction with God is effected. — Dr. Ullman. — Different Degrees of Union. — The Island Henotia described. — The Condition of human Souls symbolized by various Rivers.

WE ARE told by Plutarch that Numa, the legislator of Rome, after the death of his beloved wife, Tatia, retired into the deep forests of Aricia, and wandered in solitary musings through the thickest groves and most sequestered shades, impelled not by discontent or disgust at

26

mankind, but by an inward craving to communicate with some protecting deity. His great mind, like many other lofty intellects, pined for a divine fellowship. But he need not have buried himself in the deep gloom of the forests in order to find an every-where-present God. It is true, in those awful solitudes which never echo with the voice of man, God lives and reigns. In the deep wilderness, where the ground was never broken by the spade, where " flowers spring up unsown, and die ungathered," the purified heart may enjoy an unlonely solitude enlivened by a divine society: —

> " It is sweet
> To linger here, among the flitting birds,
> And leaping squirrels, wandering brooks, and winds
> That shake the leaves, and scatter, as they pass,
> A fragrance from the cedars, thickly set
> With pale blue berries."

God is there, for he is not subject to the limitations of time and space. He is also in the crowded city, for he is not far from every one of us. He is in that stream of living beings which flows along the noisy streets day and night. He is in the mountain. God loves the mountains. There, above the storms, man has often communed with the Invisible, and found a present Divinity. It has seemed to us, as we have stood on their lofty summits, that there was nothing there but God. Yet he is in the valley, by the side of peaceful rivers. He is on the widely-extended plain, and on the ocean, which is the image of his own eternity. And wherever we seek for him we may find him, for we are not separated from him by spatial distance, but only by a moral dissimilitude. Verily he is a God that hideth himself; but to the eye and heart of purity he manifests himself as he does not to the world. A soul in harmony with his infinite perfections will see him and enjoy him at all times and in all places. In nature he hides himself from the sensuous mind, behind the veil of second causes; but to the piercing gaze of faith, the majestic form of the Godhead is beheld through the transparent screen. It is in the deep solitude of the heart where he delights to dwell, and to reveal his presence, for the soul was made for his temple. Numa, searching for God in the forests of Aricia, stands forth the representative of many souls. The spirit of man was made capable of a state of conjunction with God, and in this alone can it find a satisfying bliss. It is characteristic of all great minds to long for communion with the infinite Creator and Father of all. But not knowing where or how to find him, they spend their life in dissatisfaction and emptiness. Their souls are like a tree withering in the sands of a desert. The experience of Augustine, so simply and eloquently described in his little book entitled Confessions, is the experience of many. He says, "I asked the earth of God, and it answered, 'I AM NOT HE.' I asked the sea and the deeps, and the living and creeping things, and they replied, 'WE ARE NOT GOD.' I asked the moving air, but the whole air, with its inhabitants, answered, 'Anaximenes was deceived; WE ARE NOT GOD.' I asked the heavens, the sun, the moon, and the stars; and they gave the same answer, but they added in the silent voice of their moving, beautiful forms, 'GOD MADE US.' O, Beauty of ancient days, ancient but ever new! Too late I sought thee; too late I found thee. I sought thee at a distance, and did not know that thou wast near. I sought thee abroad in thy works, and behold, thou wast within me."

It was the highest aim of the older systems of philosophy to teach the way in which the soul may attain to a state of conjunction with its divine Source. Their teachings were often connected with pantheistic speculations, an abyss into which the old philosophies almost invariably plunged; yet it indicates that deep craving of the soul for a union with God which is effected only in Christ and Christianity. It is interesting to observe the struggling of the primitive philosophies to reach a position of calm, unbroken repose in the bosom of Divinity. The secret yearning of the human spirit after a reunion with the Deity pervades the different systems of the Hindu philosophy. The desire to return to the ALL, and to be absorbed in the divine substance, which shows itself in those ancient systems, is but an instinctive, though perverted, longing of the human spirit for an interior and eternal unity with the Father of spirits. It needed only the light of the gospel to conduct it to the enjoyment of the highest bliss of which the soul is susceptible. It is a traditionary relic of the paradisiacal state, and a fond recollection of man's primitive condition. It breaks through the superincumbent mass of error and fable, like the old primitive rock piercing through the strata of more recent formation, and rising to the surface of the globe. Schlegel remarks, that, "in order to free themselves from transmigration, they had recourse to philosophy — to the highest aspirings of thought towards God — to a total and lasting immersion of feeling in the unfathomed abyss of the divine essence. They have never doubted that by this means a perfect union with the Deity might be obtained even in this life, and that thus the soul, freed and emancipated from all mutation and migration through the various forms of animated nature in this world of illusion, might remain forever united with God. Such is the object to which all the different systems of the Indian philosophy tend — such is the term of all their inquiries." (*Philosophy of History*, p. 160.)

They sometimes erred in looking for a union with God which should destroy the personality of the soul, the conscious self-subsistence of the creaturely spirit. The union which Christ prays the Father to grant those who should believe on him, in the future progress of his redemptive work, was a being made one with God, as he and the Father were one. He prays "that they all may be one, as thou, Father, art in me and I in thee, that they also may be one in us." (John xvii. 21.) The conjunction of God with humanity in Christ is the greatest truth in the universe, and the centre of all history. It is also the model of the union of the redeemed and regenerated spirit with the Holy One, and renders such a conjunction possible. Now, the humanity of Jesus was not made one with the Father in such a sense as would destroy its distinct personality. It was a reciprocal or mutual accession, or coming together of the two through a harmony of character and similitude of moral condition; so that, through love, they both willed one thing. Their inmost natures were sympathetic, unanimous, and concordant in every part of each. This reciprocal conjunction of the humanity of Jesus with the Father, which alone is consistent with the personality of the will of Christ, is often referred to in the teaching of Christ and his self-manifestation, which is the great miracle of the gospel. " Philip, believest thou not that I am in the Father, and the Father in me?" (John xiv.

10.) "That ye may know and believe that the Father is in me, and I in him." (John x. 38.) No other than a reciprocal union of two personalities is possible. The old Hindu philosophy placed the supreme good in "a state of abstraction by which the soul separates itself completely from nature, and even a state of annihilation, resulting from an absorption into the divine being. These were considered as states of perfect repose, supreme felicity, and the definitive object of all science." (Henry's *History of Philosophy*, vol. i. p. 60.) The annihilation here spoken of, whatever may have been the belief of a later age, was not, in all probability, viewed *originally* as a cessation of existence, for that could not have been thought a blissful state. A happy state implies the conscious existence of the spirit. It was, perhaps, no more than what Charles Wesley longed for, when he prays, —

> "O that I might now decrease!
> O that all I am might cease!
> Let me into nothing fall;
> Let my Lord be all in all."

Madame Guyon calls the highest condition of the Christian life "a profound annihilation;" not that she would have us cease to be, or lose our individuality. She would only have us aim at the destruction of what some writers on the inward life call our *proprium*, or selfhood. She would have us lose our selfish will, and would annihilate our inordinate self-love, which is the only source of evil in the universe, by the union of our wills to God.

Before the soul loses itself "in the Godhead's deepest sea," and attains the sum of all its desires, and the term of all its wanderings, in an interior spiritual union with its Source, it is usually penetrated with a profound sense of the *allness* of God and the nothingness of the creatures. It seems to me that the fundamental idea of the Scriptures, as a manifestation of the Deity, is that God is all and in all, and that God is in Christ reconciling the world unto himself. This is the central thought, around which all other ideas revolve as satellites. It is the nucleus of the Christian system around which it is organized. I can sympathize with the *feeling* of Madame Guyon, when she asserts in her profound little book, "The Short and Easy Method of Prayer," that there are only two truths in the universe — the All and the Nothing. She would not have us understand this proposition metaphysically. It expresses rather her deep sense of the greatness and infinite excellence of the all-pervading Spirit as a treasure of the soul, better, worthier, and more satisfying than all created things. It was only such a being who could quiet the vehement longings of the heart, and make it tranquil and happy. All other beings compared to him were nothing, and became of real value only in their relation to him, and their connection with the divine will. That God is all was the grand *arcanum* of the Orphic theology, according to Dr. Cudworth. Orpheus taught that "this universe and all things belonging to it were made within God; that he is the beginning, the middle, and end of all things." (*Intellectual System of the Universe*, vol. i. pp. 108–112.) The same idea is expressed by Jehovah Jesus in his manifestation to John — "I am Alpha and Omega, the beginning and the ending, the first and the last." (Rev. i. 8–11.) He is the beginning and the ending, like the first and last letters of the Greek alphabet, and consequently embraces all things in the complex. Paul declares that "for him, and through him, and to him are all things, and by him all things consist." (Rom. xi. 36. Col. i. 17.) God is all, but all things are not God. It is often but a thin and subtile line which separates truth from error. From the top of the loftiest truth, the soul sometimes plunges into the deepest abyss of falsehood. To say that the universe is God, is to utter the contradiction that the finite is the infinite. The universe, however vast it may be, can still be conceived to be greater, and hence does not answer our idea of God, who is a being so great that nothing can be conceived greater or more perfect. The universe manifests God — it was created for that end — but it does not exhibit the whole of God. There is much of God that is not in it. It does not exhaust God. The heaven, even the heaven of heavens, cannot contain him. The boundaries of creation cannot include him. To say, therefore, that created things are God, is to aver that there is no God. It is blank atheism, whatever names it may assume. All things exist *in* God. They were created within the infinite circle of the divine Mind. They are upheld by a constant exercise of the same power that formed them, so that preservation is a continued creation. Nothing exists without him. Withdraw God from any thing, and it ceases to be. Take away the substance, and the shadow which it cast disappears or is annihilated. Thus God is all and in all. He only has life in himself. All other things live by virtue of their being receptacles of his all-pervading life. What is the human soul? All its powers are the gift of God, and are the result of the divine presence. Every thing in it good and holy is an emanation from him, a ray from the Father of lights. Its continuance in existence for an hour depends upon his will. The unchanging infinite perfections of the Father of spirits, which lead him always to will only what is best, is the ground of its subsistence or continued existence. The soul could no more exist without the constant presence and power of God, than it could have originally created itself from nothing. And what is true of the soul, is true of every thing — the worm and the angel, the atom and the world. He originates and continues all other beings. They were not created from nothing, which is a contra-

diction, but from God; and they exist in him —
within the limitless area of his every where present Spirit, and the sphere of his creative activity.
He is the sea of being, and angels, and men, and
worlds are as insects floating in its depths, and we
can no more escape his presence than we can our
own. The wicked are in God by physical position,
while they are out of God and far from him by a
moral separation and dissimilitude.

The soul that is united to God is deeply pervaded with the consciousness of the *allness* of God,
and it is a soul where the indwelling Divinity has
every thing his own way — where free will, sub-
dued and taken captive by love, ceases to make
any resistance to the divine operations. There is
a state of soul, an intimate union with God, which
may be called an *annihilation*, using the term in a
qualified and not in a metaphysical sense. The
soul views God to be all, and itself and the creatures comparatively nothing, like a grain of sand
by the side of a mountain. It is not like the drop
of fresh water which descends from the cloud and
falls into the ocean, losing there its own individual
existence. It was thus viewed by Pythagoras, who

taught that the complete salvation of the soul was its transformation into God. Delivered from the multiple and variable, to use his own form of expression borrowed from his peculiar numerical philosophy, it is absorbed in the absolute unity. But the soul, annihilated in the Christian sense, still retains its individual existence. It still lives. It even exhibits the highest form of life. It is consciously living in God, having no desires out of him, and willing nothing except what he wills. It is the death of self, the transference of the soul's centre from its own contracted individual existence to God, and the separation from it of that which does not belong to its essence, but which has been acquired by the sinful activity of the will. It can adopt the sublime utterance of Paul, "I am crucified with Christ; nevertheless I live; yet not I, but Christ liveth in me." "Ye are dead, and your life is hid with Christ in God." The earthly and sensual, once the ruling element of the spirit, is now dead and buried in the grave of Christ. As the descent of Christ into the abyss corresponds to the soul's inthralment to the earthly sentiments, so the spirit's resurrection from this state of moral death is the image of Christ's ascension into the heavens. Thus speaks the apostle: "If ye be risen with Christ, seek those things which are above, where Christ sitteth on the right hand of God." (Col. iii. 1.) The old Adam expires on the cross in agony, and God in Christ alone lives in the heart. That which is peculiar to *me*, that which is not God, that which constitutes myself, which I can claim as my property, has ceased to be. The soul lives because Christ lives in it. Its life is so bound up in him that separation would be death.

> "I cannot live if thou remove,
> For thou art all in all."

It sometimes obtains so profound an immersion in the abyss of the Deity, as to lose sight of the creatures, and almost of itself. Kempis, from his own inward life, clearly apprehended this losing of ourselves in God. He says, "Dearest Jesus, Spouse of my soul, supreme Source of light and love, and sovereign Lord of universal nature! O that I had the wings of true liberty, that I might take my flight to thee and be at rest! When will it be granted me, in silent and peaceful abstraction from all created being, to taste and see how good thou art, O Lord, my God! When shall I be wholly absorbed in thy fulness? When shall I lose, in the love of thee, all perception of myself, and have no sense of any being but thine?" (*Imitation of Christ*, p. 206.)

The more intimately a soul is united to God, the more it views things as God sees them. The views and feelings of God flow into such a heart as the vital circulation of the vine pervades the branches. Submerged in the Godhead, and from the depths of God looking out upon the creatures, it sees their nothingness, and God is all. "All nations before him are as nothing; and they are counted to him as less than nothing and vanity." (Isa. xl. 17.) A soul in union and sympathy with the divine Mind thus views all created things. In heaven, God is all. The consciousness of this is one element of which heaven is made. It is an overwhelming sense of his presence that prostrates the seraph and the archangel before the throne. God is the centre of "the whole orbit of created mind." Around his throne in concentric circles they are represented in the apocalyptic vision as being arranged. Their gaze is directed inward, upon Him who sitteth upon the throne, and not outward upon the creations of God. But the redeemed of earth, in right of Him who has taken humanity up into himself, and deified it, press into the inmost circle, while angelic natures constitute the more distant circumference.

In Paradise, before sin separated man from God, the soul enjoyed the most intimate union with its Maker. Man walked with God; the perfect moral harmony between the finite and infinite Spirit prevented the painful consciousness of distance which was afterwards felt, and the two were one. It is the end of all the redeeming agencies of the gospel to bring back again to earth this original divine union. The only point in all the universe where God and man can meet is the cross of Christ. There is much emphasis in the declaration of Jesus, "I am the way, the truth, and the life; no man cometh unto the Father but by me." In him the divinity and humanity have met and become one. He has united in his person heaven and earth, God and man. Thus was he typified by the ladder which reached unto heaven, in the vision of Jacob. The soul, in entering into fellowship with the whole

Deity, must experience an interior spiritual union with Christ. Thus speaks the apostle: "Ye are dead, and your life is hid with Christ in God." The life is first concealed in Christ; then Christ, in whom we are concealed, is himself hid in God — immersed in the abyss of Deity. This is the realization in the experience of the believer of the answer of the prayer of Jesus in John xvii. 20–23. "Neither pray I for these alone, but for them also which shall believe on me through their word; that they all may be one; as thou, Father, art in me, and I in thee, that they also may be one in us; that the world may believe that thou hast sent me. And the glory which thou gavest me I have given them; that they may be one, even as we are one: I in them, and thou in me, that they may be made perfect in one." The glory which the Father gave to the Son in his humanity was a perfect union with the Divinity. This Christ has given to us. It was given to Jesus, that through him it might become the property of all who should believe on him in the future progress of the work of redemption. In this sublime prayer, he asks of God that the same union, the same perfect oneness, which subsists between him and the Father may exist between our souls and God. We should never have presumed to have asked or hoped for this, if he had not prayed for it. We should never have thought so great a dignity and blessedness to be possible for redeemed sinners, had he not declared it. But surely it cannot be deemed presumptuous in us to ask for that, which He, whom the Father always hears, has prayed that we may have. We may adopt the prayer of Jesus as our own, and with the humble boldness of faith ask that God may dwell in us, and that we may abide in him ; that we may be so joined to Christ in the unity of the same spirit, as with him to lose ourselves in God. This is like what we sometimes see symbolized in the outward world, which is full of heavenly correspondences. There is flowing onward, broad and deep, a majestic river. At a certain place a small rill rushes down from the hill side, and mingles its waters with those of the river, and both together, in one undistinguishable current, flow on to the ocean. Thus the soul is hid with Christ in God.

The *hypostatical* union, as it has been called,

by which the human nature of Christ was taken up into the divinity, has shown the possibility of the perfect union of our souls with God. We may never reach so complete a blending of the human and divine as there is in the person of Christ; yet something after the pattern of the incarnation may be ours to enjoy. Christ, in his human nature, like the first Adam, represented the whole of humanity; and when his nature was taken up into an eternal union with the Godhead, it prepared the way for the oneness or unification of our souls also with the Deity. The incarnation of Christ is the greatest truth and profoundest mystery in the universe. Why the infinite Being should feel any affinity for human nature, and any attraction towards it; why an infinite Being should love so low an object; why he should unite with any object less than infinite, — is incomprehensible. That he should take our nature up into himself, as he has done in Christ, is a love that passes knowledge. In the incarnation we see a *humanization* of the divine, in order to the *deification*, as it were, of the human. The Deity becomes a son of man that we might become sons of God. The union of the man Jesus with the divine nature prepared the way for the union of all holy souls with God, " that in the dispensation of the fulness of time he might gather together in one all things in Christ, both which are in heaven and which are on earth, even in him." (Eph. i. 10.) The apostle Paul declares that God has predestinated us unto *sonship* by Jesus Christ to himself. For when he joined that nature, which was our representative and forerunner, unto himself in an eternal union, he took our souls with it. The first fruits of this complete union with the fulness of the Godhead we may enjoy even in this life. How far the Divinity came down to meet us, and to invite us to a divine fellowship with him! He now beckons all wandering, restless souls to return to Him from whom they have revolted. O that our hearts might leap to embrace the offer, and in Jesus lose themselves in God!

The following remarks of Dr. Ullman, in his Life of Thomas à Kempis, seem to me worthy of consideration, as answering the important inquiry, how this union of the soul with God may be accomplished. " To enter into fellowship with God, the chief good and fountain of blessedness, and *to become one with him*, is the basis of all true contentment. But how can two such parties, God and man, the Creator and the creature, be brought together? God is in heaven, and man on earth; God is perfect, and man sensual, vain, and sinful. There must, therefore, be mediation, some way in which God *comes* to man, and man to God, and both unite. This union of man with God depends upon a twofold condition — one negative and the other positive. The negative is, that man shall wholly renounce what can give him no true peace. He must forsake the world, which offers to him so much hardship and distress, and whose very pleasures turn into pains; he must detach himself from the creatures, for nothing so much defiles and entangles the heart as impure love of them, and only when a man has advanced so far as no longer to seek consolation from any creature does he enjoy God, and find consolation in him; he must, in fine, die to and deny himself, and wholly renounce selfishness and self-love, for whoever loves himself will find, wherever he seeks, only his own little, mean, and sinful self, without being able to find

God. This last is the hardest of all tasks, and can only be obtained by deep self-acquaintance. But whosoever strictly exercises self-examination will infallibly come to recognize himself in his meanness, littleness, and nonentity, and will be led to the most perfect humility, entire consecration, and ardent longing after God. For only when man has become little and nothing in his own eyes can God become great to him; only when he has emptied himself of all created things can God replenish him with his grace." The positive condition also is stated: "Not only must a man become free from the world, the creatures, and himself, but God must impart himself to him, in order that he may thenceforth live to God. The two things, however, being dependent upon each other, and taking place simultaneously, cannot be effected by man alone, but are brought about essentially by God, and through divine grace." But it is well to remark that when the character of man is in harmony with God, and the human will is wholly surrendered to him, that this divine union takes place of its own accord. There is then a spiritual affinity between the divine and human. The disjunctive agency of sin in separating man from his proper centre is removed, and the soul is attracted to God and God to the soul. The only thing which disjoins the created spirit from its Creator is sin. In fact this is the only thing in the universe which is really opposed to God, and to which he is opposed. Every thing else is perfectly obedient to his will, and yields to his good pleasure. To subdue the free will of man, which has broken away in its self-activity from the orbit of perfect obedience, is the steady aim of all the moral forces of the redemptive scheme. Christianity begins here. "If any man will come after me," says Christ, "let him deny himself, and take up his cross and follow me." Plato wrote over the door of his academy, "Let no one enter here, who is ignorant of geometry." Christ has written over the gateway of the Christian system, "Except a man forsake all that he hath he cannot be my disciple." Self-renunciation is the basis of all spiritual perfection. The spirit of Gethsemane must be reproduced — a spirit which not only submits to God, but harmonizes with the divine will. The following hymn of an unknown author is pervaded with that spirit with which God always unites: —

"Prince of peace, control my will;
Bid this struggling heart be still;
Bid my fears and doubtings cease;
Hush my spirit into peace.

Thou hast bought me with thy blood,
Opened wide the gate to God:
Peace I ask, but peace must be,
Lord, in being one with thee.

May thy will, not mine, be done;
May thy will and mine be one;
Chase these doubtings from my heart;
Now thy perfect peace impart.

Saviour, at thy feet I fall;
Thou my life, my God, my all:
Let thy happy servant be
One forevermore with thee."

A soul in such a moral attitude may, consistently with the divine perfections, be met of God and blessed with the divine presence. When the barrier of a selfish, sinful will is removed, the infinite and finite spirits flow into one. The moral harmony of nature which constitutes the ground of the union of the soul to God, may exist in different degrees. In its lowest degree it may be only a union of desires. The soul desires what is pleasing to God. Though conscious of many defects and blemishes of spirit which must be offensive to the Holy One, it inwardly yearns for full conformity to the divine likeness. It may, in addition, and as a more advanced stage, love what God loves, and hate what he hates. In its affections it may sympathize with God. But the union is only complete when the will is restored to that harmony with the divine will which was its original state. Then the blissful familiarity between God and his creature, which was the chief element of the paradisiacal state, is restored. "For thus saith the high and lofty One that inhabiteth eternity, whose name is Holy: I dwell in the high and holy place, with him also that is of a humble and contrite spirit, to revive the spirit of the humble, and to revive the heart of the contrite ones." (Isa. lvii. 15.)

Man, by the depraved activity of his will, has broken away from God. He has forsaken God, but God has not forsaken him. Man must, therefore, return to him. It is in accordance with the laws of divine order, which the Deity has established, and which are as invariable as the infinite perfections of Jehovah, from which they proceed, that man must return unto God, and prepare himself for the reception of God; and so far as he does this will God enter into him, as into his habitation and house. Man must accede or approach unto God; and then will God accede or approach unto man, according to the promise, "Draw nigh unto God, and he will draw nigh unto thee." (James iv. 8.) "Return unto me, and I will return unto you, saith the Lord of hosts." (Mal. ii. 7.) This we are to do, in the exercise of our free will, as from ourselves, though the grace, which empowers us so to act, is from Him who is the fountain of every good and perfect gift.

In the Island of Henotia, the centre of the group of the Happy Islands, the soul attained the end of its creation. Its life became mingled with the current of the divine life in Christ, and flowed on with it. This island was larger than any of the others. The others seemed to have been separated from it. In the centre there stood a mountain covered with perpetual verdure, surrounded with several lesser summits. The water flowed down from these hills, in beautiful cascades, into a small central lake, where they all united. Between two hills there was presented a vale of surpassing beauty, some three miles in length, and which was called "the Vale of Repose" — *Vallis Quietis*. The small river, proceeding from the lake, flowed through this valley, and after passing through a plain enamelled with flowers, discharged its waters into the ocean. The valley extended on each side of the river nearly a mile. It was adorned with the beautiful creations of God. The atmosphere was serene, and the hills crowned with herbage to their summits. Along the banks of this river, the Divine Man walked with the soul. The inhabitants of the island, clothed in garments white as the unsullied snow, might be seen on the hill sides and in the vale. A place of such divine blessedness was never before seen on earth. Here the soul found all that it had lost in the original transgression, and here it resolved to make its abode while it remained on earth. From this place it would send out an invitation to all the struggling souls of earth to come and share its perfect blessedness.

Here it appeared more clearly than had ever before been realized, that the proper destination of a human soul is an eternal union with God, through the mediation of Christ, just as a river flows onward, until it mingles its waters with those of the abyss. But there are some rivers which empty into lakes, and do not reach the ocean directly. They appear satisfied to lose themselves in some inland sea, instead of flowing onward to the great deep, which is their proper destination, and whence they came. So there are souls that seek their supreme good only in the enjoyment of earthly things. They are of the earth, earthy : —

> "Yet man, fool man, here buries all his thoughts,
> Inters celestial hopes, without one sigh ;
> Prisoner of earth, and pent beneath the moon,
> Here pinions all his wishes, winged of Heaven
> To fly at infinite, and reach it there
> Where seraphs gather immortality
> On life's fair tree, fast by the throne of God."

There are other rivers, which, after flowing for a long distance, are absorbed by the sands of the desert, or what is worse, discharge themselves into stagnant marshes, the home of dragons and all loathsome reptiles. These dismal marshes load every breeze with their death-dealing malaria. They represent a class of human souls — men who lose all sense of God, and relish for divine things, carnal, earthly, selfish, whose influence is a moral pestilence. All their thoughts, hopes, affections, and desires are buried in the stagnant slough of sensuality. But the largest and noblest rivers never rest until they reach the ocean. Some of them flow thousands of miles before they discharge their waters into the sea; running onward, night and day, between the mountains and the hills, through the valleys and plains, traversing whole empires before they become one with the ocean. Sometimes they lose themselves in the abyss noiselessly and quietly. They make no resistance, and without a struggle mingle their waters with the waves of the deep, and soon partake of all the properties and qualities of the sea, reposing, after all their wanderings, in its bosom. But sometimes, at the point where a vast river, which has flowed through kingdoms, and which is proud of its independence, comes in contact with the ocean, there is a terrible commotion, like the hostile commingling of heaven and earth. The river dies hard. It is unwilling to lose itself and be merged in the abyss. It clings, with a convulsive death grasp, to its self hood. The ocean goes calmly forth to meet it, but it repels the embrace, and shrinks back upon itself. Travellers have spoken of the terrific spectacle produced when the tide of the Atlantic meets the current of the Amazon. It is like the conflict of Titans, the war of giants. The earth trembles with the roar of their blows, and man flies with terror from the scene of the encounter. At length, however, the river yields, the ocean conquers, — for what is the mightiest river compared with the ocean? — the war ceases, and they are locked in a perpetual embrace. So there are souls that quietly and calmly resign their will to God. They sink, by dying love compelled, and without a struggle plunge into the " Godhead's deepest sea," and lose themselves in his immensity, and sleep on the abyss of Deity, which is without a surge. They make no more resistance than midnight does to the noiseless approach of the morning. There are others, who, right at the point of parting with all that they may gain all, pass through a terrible struggle. The old nature dies hard. The nails and thorns of the cross hurt. The soul is convulsed like the upheaving of mountains. But when, in this struggle of free will against the demands of God, which he ceaselessly thunders in our ears, the heart cries, —

> "Nay, but I yield, I yield;
> I can hold out no more,"

the contest is ended. Our selfhood dies. Our will yields to the current of the divine attraction, and loses itself in God. We are then dead, and our life is hid with Christ in God.

We have now made the circuit of the Happy Islands, and glanced at the blessedness of their inhabitants. But never can it fully be comprehended except by an actual residence there. Let me then urge my Christian friend, who has deigned to read this little volume, to start at once in search of them. They are not afar off, but near at hand. The voyage to them is neither difficult nor perilous. Unless you are driven out of your course, or deceived by outward appearances, or stop at some land which is not the region of the blessed, you may soon reach them. Paradise has not been forever lost to earth. The Redeemer has opened wide its gates, and invites us to enter. If we live in a wilderness of sin and woe, it is not because Christianity has been meagre in its provisions. Christ has provided a salvation as finished as our ruin was complete. Let us avail ourselves of the ample provisions of his redeeming scheme, and find rest in the cross of Christ.

"Come, Holy Ghost, all-quickening fire,
Come, and in me delight to rest;
Drawn by the lure of strong desire,
O, come and consecrate my breast;
The temple of my soul prepare,
And fix thy sacred presence there.

If now thine influence I feel,
If now in thee begin to live,
Still to my heart thyself reveal;
Give me thyself, forever give;
A point my good, a drop my store,
Eager I ask, I pant for more.

Eager for thee I ask and pant;
So strong the principle divine
Carries me out with sweet constraint,
Till all my hallowed soul is thine;
Plunged in the Godhead's deepest sea,
And lost in thy immensity.

My peace, my life, my comfort thou,
My treasure and my all thou art;
True witness of my sonship, now
Engraving pardon on my heart;
Seal of my sins in Christ forgiven,
Earnest of love, and pledge of heaven."